SPICE MEN

Edited By

MARCUS ANTHONY

Herndon, VA

ISBN 13: 978-1-61303-017-2

Published in the United States by STARbooks Press

PO Box 711612, Herndon, VA 20171

Many thanks to graphic artist Emma Aldous:
www.arthousepublishing.co.uk

Printed in the United States

Herndon, VA

Titles by Marcus Anthony

The Sweeter the Juice

Tall, Dark & Delicious

Spice Men

Black Dungeon Masters

CONTENTS

TAKING CHANCES
By Evan Gilbert

They left the movie theater, two very tall, very good-looking black men on a date. Dahn Stewart was six-foot-six, a dark-skinned twenty-four-year-old with a face that could only be described as beautiful – deep brown eyes, elegantly shaped nose, thin, neat black mustache over firm, slender lips, dimpled cheeks. His muscled body was sleek and lean. Ajamu Jones was just as tall, but his build was thicker with muscle, his skin a few shades lighter, his face more rugged in its attractiveness. Where Dahn's scalp boasted a closely trimmed, carefully lined afro, Ajamu's head was gloriously bald. There was no physical contact between them – they each had their hands shoved into the pockets of their loose-fitting jeans as they walked – but it was obvious to everyone around them that they were unabashedly into each other.

They met on Ajamu's first visit to the midtown health spa where Dahn had long been a member, their mutual attraction established the instant their eyes met across a main floor crowded with fitness machines spread out like rows of giant, stationary, armored insects. Ajamu had grown up in the inner city, reared by a strict, widowed, father who held him on a tight leash despite working two jobs to support them. That tight leash kept Ajamu away from gangs and got him through college, a fact he had only recently come to realize and appreciate. At twenty-six, Ajamu was one month away from completing his doctorate. A position as a pharmacist was awaiting him at the Methodist University Hospital the moment that degree was in his hands, and he was house-hunting in the suburbs, ready to settle down in more ways than one. He was tired of one-night stands. He wanted a partner, a man to share his life.

He wanted Dahn.

Dahn's life, it seemed, had turned upside down. He had grown up in an upper middle-class home, his parents providing him with every comfort and demanding academic achievement in return. He held a bachelor's degree in social work and a job as an investigator with the state's Child Protective Services Agency, but three years of dealing with horribly abused kids, and the monsters who hurt them, had left him burned out. He wanted desperately to move on to something else. Moreover, he was only six weeks out of an ugly, two-year relationship with a chronically unfaithful lover. His feelings were still raw, and the last thing he needed now was to be hurt again. Yes, Ajamu was fine as hell, but that meant he would have no problem picking up guys whenever and wherever he wanted. Dahn couldn't lower his guard. This was his third date with Ajamu in the two weeks since they'd met, and he still had not allowed so much as a kiss between them.

The spring Saturday afternoon was sunny and warm. They ambled across Overton Square, a collection of shops, bars and restaurants in sprawling Memphis, Tennessee, that was a smaller, more sedate version of New Orleans' French Quarter. Dahn was more at ease now, finally shaking off the stress of a hectic work week. The movie had been funny, and he was enjoying himself.

"So, you a fan of the Rock?" Ajamu asked, referring to the star of the movie they had just seen.

"I like some of his flicks. I don't get the sex-symbol hype, though."

"You mean he doesn't stir your juices?"

"No, but you want to know who does? Kirk Franklin."

"The little no-singing, wanna-be-rapper gospel dude?" Ajamu asked incredulously.

"Yeah, man. I like full lips, and that brother's got one of the prettiest set of blowers on earth." Dahn had developed a crush on the performer after seeing him in concert seven years ago. "I'd be ashamed to tell you the things I imagine Brother Kirk doing to me with those lips."

"You don't believe in God, do you?"

"Of course I do. Why would you think I'm an atheist?"

"'Cause saying what you just did about God's littlest messenger would have a Christian man looking over his shoulder for lightning bolts."

Dahn laughed. "What about you? If you could have a celebrity, who would it be?"

The corners of Ajamu's mouth turned down in a facial shrug. "Well, if we go back a ways, I'd take dude from Soul Food, the series ..."

"Boris Kodjoe?"

"Nah. Darrin Dewitt Henson."

"That's a hot brother," Dahn agreed.

"And Bow Wow."

"Lil' Mr. Shad Moss, the rapper, oh, yeah. Very nice face."

"Taylor Lautner."

"Taylor Lautner?"

"Hey, you get a good look at him in those *Twilight* movies? That's a fine, pretty-ass white boy."

"There is nothing a white man can do for me in the bedroom."

Ajamu placed his right hand patriotically over his heart. "Well, I'm an equal opportunity fucker. Black, brown, white – long as a dude's got a fine butt, I'll poke him."

A thirtyish woman, strolling along ahead of the two men, turned and gave them a long, offended stare.

Ajamu returned the look. "What, lady? You wouldn't fuck Taylor Lautner?"

The woman hurried off in disgust.

"Must be a dyke," Dahn said.

It was only 5:05 pm, much too early to drive out to the nightclub Ajamu had selected for the second part of their date. They returned to Dahn's townhouse. "I've got the new Fourplay CD," Dahn said after inviting Ajamu to take a seat on the sofa. Ajamu was very much into smooth jazz.

"Hey, let's hear that, man." Ajamu watched as Dahn crossed to the entertainment center against the opposite wall and knelt down to load a disk into the CD player. When Dahn was finished, soft jazz began pouring into the room. He stood up and turned, catching Ajamu's stare.

"What?"

"You're one strange motherfucker," said Ajamu.

"I'm strange."

"Yeah. You're like ..." Ajamu's eyes turned upward as his mind searched for words. "You're out there, bruh. Deep space. Where no man has gone before. Every time we get together, seems like part of you is missing. You got secrets."

"And you don't?" Dahn said, seating himself on the sofa next to Ajamu.

Ajamu smiled slowly in response. "I like you. There're folk out there who ain't about shit. But you're about something. You got your own place, your own car. You're holdin' down a job. You got goals. Plus, you're fine as hell."

Dahn was pleased with the compliment but dismissed it, unwilling to let Ajamu know he had just scored a point. "And that's what counts, huh? Being fine."

"Shoot. It doesn't hurt." He paused. "I can't stop thinking about you, man. That's scary."

The words gave Dahn a jolt of fear, so sharp that he couldn't respond. They sat for a time listening to the music. Ajamu reached out and traced a fingertip along Dahn's forearm, enjoying the silky feel of that richly dark skin. Taking Dahn's hand, he rose. "Dance with me."

Dahn froze, as he always did when things began to get physical between the two of them. But he knew that if he continued pushing Ajamu away, the man would eventually move on, and rightfully so.

Time to step out on faith, Dahn thought, quoting the words his mother had used when he was afraid to make a certain move.

Dahn stood up. Ajamu wrapped his arms around him, pulling him in. Ajamu tried to lead and Dahn, with a mischievous grin, playfully resisted. It was Ajamu who yielded, resting his chin on Dahn's shoulder and letting himself be guided slowly across the floor. His left hand came up, fingers first massaging Dahn's neck, then tracing the outline of his ear. Dahn loved the sensation, surprised by the man's tenderness. He responded by running a hand firmly up Ajamu's spine and kissing his neck.

"That feels good, man," Ajamu moaned in his ear.

Ajamu slid his right hand along Dahn's waist. Dahn grabbed Ajamu's head and tilted it back, leaning forward to brush his lips lightly across the other man's mouth. Ajamu could feel

Dahn's excitement against his thigh and felt himself growing hard in response. He slipped his right hand into Dahn's back pocket and squeezed a beefy cheek.

Dahn moaned deeply, closing his eyes, but rather than melt into the embrace, he began to pull away. Ajamu tried to hold him in, tightening his grip on Dahn's body. Dahn slipped out of Ajamu's arms, looking into his eyes with an intensity that shone both hunger and fear. Ajamu stepped toward him. Dahn shook his head, backing further away.

"You want me to go?" Ajamu asked, confused.

"Hell no, man. I'm enjoying your company." Dahn was silent for a moment, taking swift, deep breaths as if he had just finished an all-out run. "Damn. You want something to drink? I could use a little something ..."

"I'll get it, bruh. What you got in the kitchen?"

"Just a six-pack of Pepsi in the fridge."

Ajamu walked toward the kitchen, and Dahn's eyes followed, locked on the roundness of the man's buttocks flexing sensuously beneath the draping denim of his jeans. Dahn exhaled loudly and closed his eyes.

The Jazz Royale was a sprawling, split-level nightclub housed in a converted movie theater on the northeastern corner of Beale and Fourth downtown. In Our Image, the seven-member band commanding the stage that Saturday night poured out a barrage of Latin-tinged jazz with a driving beat. The dance floor below the stage was already packed with shaking, spinning bodies when Ajamu and Dahn arrived just after eight.

The music captured Ajamu instantly. He grabbed Dahn's wrist and tugged him toward the stage. The extemporaneous nature of the act struck Dahn as uncommonly bold, and he found his respect for Ajamu growing. As they moved onto the dance floor, Dahn realized they were far from being the only two men dancing together. The club's patronage appeared to be largely heterosexual and white, but there were a surprising number of same-sex couples about, and their presence garnered not so much as a second glance.

Ajamu swung into a Salsa that incorporated the laid-back, shoulder shaking, head bopping bounce of hip-hop. Dahn, never having danced the Salsa, was largely motionless, mesmerized by the sheer masculinity of Ajamu's muscular body in motion. He groaned when Ajamu turned his back to him, jeans riding low on his hips and clinging smoothly to the upper lobes of his curved, brawny rump. Dahn fought the rising urge to slide his own body in close to the man's swaying butt. Ajamu turned around and, seeing the uncertainty in Dahn's moves, reached out and grabbed Dahn's hips. His insistent hands guided Dahn's body into the dance. Within seconds, Dahn was moving in synch with Ajamu's blithe steps.

The pulsing tempo of the music filled Dahn with an ardor that was urgent and unrelenting. That led him to dance with abandon, riding the crest of each beat in a frenzy that only increased the passions surging inside him. Twice Ajamu tried to lead him off the floor, and Dahn yanked himself away each time, unwilling to stop.

Finally, more than an hour later, Dahn felt the anxiety abruptly seeping away, and he staggered off the floor with Ajamu following closely behind. Dahn found an empty spot along the wall and propped his back against it, his head, neck and chest wet with perspiration.

"Damn, bruh," Ajamu said breathlessly. "You can move."

Dahn smiled at him. "I think I'm ready to go home."

Ajamu returned the smile. "Okay. Let's go."

Once they were in Ajamu's SUV, Dahn put his head back and closed his eyes. By the time they reached his townhouse, he was half-asleep. Ajamu put a hand on Dahn's knee and gently shook him awake. "You're home, man."

Ajamu followed Dahn to the front steps, waiting patiently while Dahn dug his keys out of his pocket and unlocked the door. Dahn turned to look at him, loving the attractiveness of Ajamu's sweat-streaked face and the clear reluctance to leave in those wide brown eyes. He could see the erection bulging down the left leg of Ajamu's jeans, as stark and dangerous as a weapon, and despite the exhaustion in his own body, he felt himself responding in kind. And again he felt an undefined fear whispering around the edges of that desire.

"I'm really tired," he mumbled.

Ajamu nodded slowly but could not keep the disappointment out of his eyes. "All right, man. I had a good time with you today. We gotta do this again, real soon."

"I hear ya, man. I enjoyed being with you, too. Thanks." Dahn leaned forward, brushing a soft kiss across Ajamu's thick lips. "Be careful driving home."

"Yeah. See ya."

Dahn stood in his doorway until Ajamu climbed into the SUV and drove off. He closed and bolted the door. He stood there, touching a finger to his mouth, where the feel of Ajamu's kiss still lingered. He flicked out his tongue, tasting the saltiness left by the man's lips. He closed his eyes, seeing the man's wet, hot, glistening, handsome-as-hell face.

Damn ...

His hand slid down the front of his jeans.

In his mind, in his dreams, he once again faced Ajamu on the doorstep after parting from their kiss. Only, instead of sending the big, gorgeous man away, he would throw open the door, grab the front of Ajamu's shirt, yank him inside and kick the door shut.

"Dang, man," Ajamu would drawl through that sweet, lazy smile of his. "Look at you, goin' all butch on a brother."

One of Dahn's eyes popped open suddenly. "Okay, maybe Ajamu wouldn't use the word 'butch,'" he admitted aloud, shaking his head.

Still, that little glitch wasn't going to derail his fantasy, to which he returned upon closing his eyes again. His response to whatever Ajamu said would be to plant his hands on the man's shoulders and shove him down on the sofa. He'd begin ravenously kissing Ajamu, devouring those rich, full lips, savoring the salty-sweet taste of them over and over again. He'd force Ajamu's legs apart, pressing their crotches together, grinding one denim-covered dick against another.

Then his attention would go to Ajamu's neck, where he would lick away the drying sweat and then start nibbling, leaving hickies all up and down the light-brown skin there.

"Man ... man ..." Ajamu would mutter eagerly, again and again.

Dahn would grab Ajamu's T-shirt, yanking it up and off his torso, then rip the jeans open and snatch them away, leaving the man wearing nothing but his big, black and red sneaks. Dahn would drown in the sight of Ajamu's hard chest, six-pack abs, and big, muscular legs as he stripped away his own clothes, and Ajamu would stare helplessly up at him, waiting.

Once out of his clothes, Dahn would not hesitate. His head would plunge down between Ajamu's legs, his tongue lapping along the thick length of the prominently-veined, uncut cock there. Like the rest of Ajamu's body, the cock would taste of a steamy brininess. Dahn would nibble at the head, dabble it with kisses, before sucking the dick into his mouth and down his throat. Ajamu would give a loud, surprised groan of pleasure, his thick thighs clamping tightly around Dahn's head, drawing the clutching lips all the way down to the fat round base of his cock. Dahn would bob up and down on that cock for several long, delightful minutes, his mouth sucking hungrily, getting Ajamu hotter and hotter.

And then, just when the big dick was on the verge of spurting, Dahn would pull away, grab Ajamu's knees and push them up to the man's chest, rolling that big, round booty up and open. He would let his tongue trail slowly up and down the deep, hairy crack of Ajamu's ass. Then he'd work a finger, gently but deliberately, down between those marvelous mounds, seeking out the tiny little bud within. He'd rub his finger over Ajamu's asshole, probing it, teasing it, while it sucked at his finger, urging him in.

The groans coming from Ajamu would be loud ... hot ... desperate. "Do it, Dahn. Fuck, man, do it!"

There'd be no more games then, no more teasing.

Dahn would roll on a condom, then get Ajamu's ass good and wet with lube.

Dahn would hitch Ajamu's legs over his shoulders.

Dahn would grab his own big, hard, aching dick and plunge it into Ajamu's waiting and willing body. He would fuck Ajamu hard and deep, his dark cock sliding in and out of that hot, hairy, tight brown ass. Ajamu would throw his head back, eyes rolling up, as deep, sexy groans poured out of his throat. He wouldn't be able to move, wouldn't be able to do anything but lie there with his long, thick body bent double and take it. Dahn would pound the fuck out of that ass, would dick that hole down until …

His eyes popped open. He was leaning forward, his right hand propped against the door. His jeans were down to his ankles, his left hand jerking away at his cock. He was about to come.

He stopped.

You could have the real thing, he told himself. *All it would take is a phone call. Ajamu's not home yet. And even if he were, he'd come back in a hot second if you asked him to.*

He wanted more than just sex. He wanted Ajamu to wake up with him in the morning, wanted them to make breakfast together and see where a free and open Sunday would take them. He realized as well that he could fall, deeply and hard, for this man. And that brought the fear rising so quickly into his head yet again that it leeched the heat right out of his body. His dick began to droop.

But hell, what was life if not a series of chances?

He pulled up his pants and hauled out his cell phone. As he dialed, he pictured Ajamu's fine brown face. He could feel the heat going back into his groin again.

The call was answered after the second ring. "Hey, man." Ajamu's thick, happy voice made Dahn's heart jump. "I was just thinking about you. Whassup?"

"Get your ass back here," Dahn said. "That's what's up."

"Oh, shit. Here I come, baby ..."

SPICE BOYS
By Logan Zachary

"Tell me what you want, what you really really want." I flopped down on the chair and picked up the stack of men's photos and bios.

"Cute, but the new boy group will be amazing. Once we get the concept right, I'm sure we can market them." Sam turned over one head shot and read the bio on the back.

"That's why my idea is a sure thing."

"The Spice Boys?" He scoffed.

"It worked for the girls ..." I started.

"And where are they now?"

"One is married to an underwear model and a professional soccer player, oh so sexy."

"She's a robot, or so the gossip rags say. And the others?" He turned to look at me. His deep blue eyes bore into my brown ones and melted my balls.

I picked up one picture and showed him. "Here's JockStrap Spice. Imagine him dancing in just a cup and an elastic band. His dark brown skin contrasting against a white jock, or red? Or yellow? What do you think?"

He licked his lips and puckered up to kiss him. "I can see it in my mind's eye, an amazing ass, with deep rich chocolate skin."

"Exactly." My dick started to swell with the images that danced in my mind. A deep throbbing beat, my heart and the music mixed to increase my blood flow.

"Are you getting off on this?" One of Sam's hands slipped underneath the table to adjust himself.

"Hell, yes, aren't you?" I noticed his arm motion. "Are you playing with yourself under the table?"

His hands flew above the table and landed with a bang. His face flushed as he bit his lower lip.

I glanced at the clock in the studio's sound room. "They should be here any minute."

"Who?"

"The Spice Boys."

"Seriously?"

"Well, that's not what they're called right now, but if we can work it out, I'm sure they'll do an album and videos as needed. They're hungry and good. It shouldn't be hard for them to breakout out on the Billboard charts."

A knock came on the door, I rose and opened it. Five black men in various shades of skin tones entered and lined up. "Come on in guys. This is Sam. He's the record producer, and we're trying to convince him to run with the Spice Boys idea."

The men nodded at Sam, who stared opened mouthed at them.

The darkest man was husky and looked like a body builder. He stepped forward and said, "I'm James," with his rich smoky voice.

I sat back in my seat and pulled his bio out of the pile and handed it to Sam.

As Sam read it, he asked, "Are you guys okay with the Spice Boys theme?"

James smiled, "We've been looking for a name for our group, and if it gets us a deal, we'll be anyone you want us to be from the new black Village People, the Five Tops, the Temptations, or the Mandingos."

Sam swallowed hard. James was beautiful and eloquent.

I rifled through the other head shots and pulled them out as I found them. "Nigel is from England." The man with spring loaded dreds stepped forward. He had a short compact body with powerful legs. "Jeffrey has sung backup for Prince, Sheila E, and Janet Jackson." A tall slender model stepped forward, his dark complexion shown in the spotlight, his white even smile. He raised his long arm and waved at Sam.

"Dominic stripped for Thunder Down Under, and Ken sang in the cast of *Ragtime* on Broadway."

Dominic pulled his shirt open to show a sculpted body of a golden brown, as Ken dropped to one knee and raised his arms up over his head.

"Can they sing?" Sam asked.

I inserted a CD into the player. "Are you ready boys?" I hit play and the music started. The men started moving with the music, each moved independent of the others, but slowly all fell into sync with each other. Their motions perfect with the beat of the music.

Dominic unbuttoned his shirt as he grooved and rocked his narrow hips back and forth. As the last button released, he tossed his shirt to the side. Jeffrey pulled his form fitting T-shirt over his head and showed his glistening muscles. James unzipped his running suit and a hairy chest came into view.

Nigel's hair bounced like springs on his head as he danced in place. His shirt slipped off easily and fluttered to the floor. Ken wore a wife beater, and he ripped it down the front as he gyrated his hips.

As the shirtless men sang, their voices blended into harmonies and melodies that sent Goosebumps over Sam's and my bodies. Their muscles rippled under the smooth skin on their torsos. Each shade was a unique tone for the men.

I felt my erection start to grow again, filling with blood as each pelvis thrust in our direction. Tight jeans hugged their ass, huge baskets stood out in the front of the men as they moved as one.

As I watched their bulges, I missed them kicking off their shoes. As they danced barefoot, I held my breath as they started to undo their flies.

Sam's hand grabbed my arm and squeezed. "Are they going to …" He licked his dry lips and was unable to continue.

"Watch," was all I could say.

James untied the knot in his waistband, and the elastic loosen. White Vs appeared on the other four's groins. Underwear strained with what they contained.

My hard-on itched and ached to be released from my tight pants, too.

Sam crossed his legs as if he had to go to the restroom. One of his hands disappeared back underneath the table, but I didn't say anything this time. Mine joined his, but in my crotch.

One by one, the singers removed their pants and danced only in white bikini briefs. The black lights made their underwear glow as their cocks were easily outlined in the sheer cotton.

These men had the moves and the voices to go far. I had struck gold with this find, and Sam knew it, too.

Each man on stage turned and swung his booty from side to side. The cotton ran up their creases and hugged their bubble butts. Sweat made the fabric see-through and hug each curve.

James looked over his shoulder and said, "If you wanna be my lover, you gotta get with my friends." He waved for Sam and me to join them. He pulled one side of his briefs down to flash us one fleshy cheek. Perfect, brown, and round.

I could feel my cock push against my pants. I opened the clasp and pulled the zipper back slightly. My hand caressed the bump, and I felt moisture soak into my underwear. I shook my head.

Each man pulled his underwear down on the right cheek and slapped the bare flesh. They ground their hips around and repeated the unveiling on the other cheek. Their full moons glowed on each guy as they swung their hips side to side. They bent forward and pushed their underwear down to their feet.

As they rose to upright, they lifted their left feet out of the briefs and stepped to the side. With their other legs, they kicked and sent the bikinis sailing away. A few low hanging balls swung freely between their legs.

Singing over their shoulders, they grabbed their cocks and covered themselves, as they spun to face us.

My hand worked my erection, waiting for the full Monty to appear.

They swayed from side to side and thrust their pelvises forward.

Jeffrey raised his hands and let his long slender dick flap back and forth.

I wrote "Licorice" by his name.

Dominic raised his hands and swayed his hips. His thick cock twirled like a propeller.

"Caramel" scratched across the page.

Nigel's dark skin rippled in the lights and as he spread his arms, a thick penis waved at us.

"Cocoa."

Ken mirrored Nigel's motions, and his lighter skin tones greeted me.

"Vanilla."

I licked my lips and inhaled deeply. Male sweat and sex filled the room, the temperature rose as did the humidity.

James moved forward at the center of the men and brought his hands up. He was hung like a horse. His huge cock stood straight out and bobbed up and down. Wetness appeared at the tip. The girth looked like a beer can from where I sat.

"Horseradish" was all I could come up with.

Sam's breathing was coming in short and quick bursts. Was he jacking off or hyperventilating?

I reached over and touched his arm and felt him jump. He turned to me and gasped. "What the fuck?"

"I know. They'll be huge."

"They are HUGE!"

"Told you."

Jeffrey moved behind Dominic and wrapped his arms around him. He slid his cock between his cheeks and slipped it up and down his crack. One of his long arms reached around and grasped his semi-hard cock. He stroked it and worked to a full blown erection.

Ken did the same thing to Nigel, whose cock grew to even larger than I had initially seen. Ken rode Nigel's ass and felt his dick swell and grow as he probed for an opening.

James stepped forward and approached our table. His erection grew and grew as it came closer to us. Sam's body slammed back in his seat as his hand frantically worked under the table.

I leaned forward, and James stopped. His raging stallion hovered over the table. A pearly cream bead formed at the tip and slowly dripped down and out. His hairy balls brushed the table's surface and settled on the surface.

I reached across the table. My fingers brushed the wetness away and smeared it around the black mushroom end. My hand slipped down his warm, meaty shaft and brushed into his thick curly bush. My finger trailed down to his massive balls and cupped them, feeling the heavy weight of them. Plums were smaller than his testicles.

Sam slapped my ass. "Go for it."

James stroked my face and inserted a finger into my mouth. I sucked on it. His low husky voice said, "What's our friendship for? My friends and I like to play, come join us." He turned to Sam. "And you're invited, too." He spun around, shook his black booty and raised one leg to rest on the table, spreading his backside wide open.

I looked behind James and saw Dominic was on his knees and Jeffrey was working on his beautiful butt. Ken rode Nigel, and his moans of pleasure replaced the singing with an even more heavenly sound.

"Spice up your life." James grabbed my wrist and pulled me around the table.

I stumbled after him and felt my pants start to slip down my ass with each step. My hard-on pushed the zipper lower and loosened the pants even more. I grabbed them before they hit the floor and tripped me.

James' hand slid into my pants and squeezed my ass. "Not bad for a white boy."

I jumped at his touch.

"Strip down and get naked. We're giving you everything we got."

Dominic and Nigel reached out for us and waved us closer. Dominic licked his lips and puckered up.

Nigel said, "We enjoy playing and singing together." He slapped his ass.

I felt my body being lead into the center of the space where they had sung. Hands pulled on my clothes, unbuttoning and unzipping, the nubile natives surrounding their prey and readied to eat me, alive.

My body was naked, and as the men stepped forward, I could feel the heat that radiated off them and into me. I was the filling of an Oreo. A damp palm slid down my ass as a finger traced my crease. Another hand pulled my other cheek, and I could feel my pucker expose to the air.

"Flawless porcelain," Nigel dropped to his knees and buried his face between my cheeks. His thick, rough tongue found my tender opening and swirled around and around, his tip seeking entry as he savored my favor.

23

Jeffery stepped in front of me and guided my head down to his long slender cock. As he rubbed the tip over my lips, I swore I tasted licorice.

Ken and Dominic nodded to each other and motioned over to the table where Sam still sat. They pulled out of our circle jerk and headed in his direction.

"Loosen him up for me," James said into my ear. He thrust his dick into my hand.

Instinctively, my fingers wrapped around his girth, and I couldn't touch on the other side. His cock was moist and slipped easily along my palm.

I felt a warm, thick fluid spill over my fingers and spread along his length.

He gave out a low moan as his hips humped my fist.

Jeffrey's licorice whip entered my mouth and worked slowly, deeper down my throat. It seemed to swell as it went down.

Just add water flashed through my mind, and I coughed, as I lost my concentration on sucking him.

Nigel's saliva dripped from between my cheeks and ran down my hairy legs. I could feel his tongue lick my balls, my pucker, and along my crack. His tongue tried to enter me, and I relaxed my muscles as the tip slipped in. The scent of cocoa filled my nostrils, and I breathed in deeply. Yes, it was Nigel. He would be Cocoa Spice. My mouth watered from the rich smell of dark chocolate.

James knelt down by Nigel and added his mouth and tongue. James thick cock slapped my toes, and I felt the weight of his meat. Precum oozed out of the end and ran over the bridge of my foot. He was hung like a horse and Horseradish Spice seemed perfect.

Jeffrey pulled my head back and kissed me deeply. His tongue tasted mine, and when he broke the kiss he asked, "Black licorice?"

"It's what you taste like. Spicy and delicious."

He pulled my head to his mouth, seeking mine with his tongue, while he worked his magic. He pushed me down to my knees.

I glanced over at the table. Sam lay across the table, naked. His butt hung over the edge, and Ken's dick was buried deep inside his ass. Dominic's huge cock was slipping in and out of his mouth. Sam's hands worked his erection, making his testicles bounce up and down.

I enjoyed watching Sam being spit roasted, and my body longed for the same treatment. I felt James push Nigel out of the way and stepped between my legs and rub his horse cock up and down my crease. His fat mushroom head was a deep red, and he guided it between my cheeks. Saliva and precum made my ass slick. How I wanted James inside me, but I doubted he'd fit.

Nigel moved around me and grabbed my cock. He slid it into his mouth and sucked it in inch by glorious inch. He deep throated me until my balls pressed against his chin. His hands reached around me and pulled my hips to him. He spread my cheeks apart, and James inserted a thick finger into me.

Jeffrey stood above Nigel and fed his dick into my mouth. Licorice danced across my taste buds, and I swallowed.

James added another finger inside me and stretched me wider and wider. He wiggled them inside me, loosening me, relaxing me, preparing me.

I started to protest, but James' large hand stroked my bare back and soothed me. "Relax, enjoy the ride." He slowed his pace in and out of me, twisting his hand and fingers as he explored me.

Jeffrey's cock tasted so good in my mouth. He pressed it in as far as it would go, and I swallowed and sucked on him.

Nigel's tongue worked his way up and down my shaft. His springing dreads tickled my belly as he savored my juices.

I managed to gurgle out, "There's lube and condoms in the top drawer."

James pulled his hand out of my butt and grabbed his erection. He slipped on an x-large condom and lubed it up.

I knew what he was planning, and my ass tensed up.

James large hands grabbed my hips as his thumbs opened my cheeks. He aimed his hard-on at my hole and surged forward.

I felt the huge penis plow my row and find my hole. It rubbed the sweet spot and pushed in. The sensation on my cock and the one in my mouth warmed me from the core. My body wanted it inside me, and I pressed back. I felt my pucker loosen as my hips rocked back and forth, each backward thrust swallowed James' monster millimeter by millimeter.

The pressure built, and the stretching almost became painful, but with one deep breath, I relaxed and I felt him slip inside.

James paused for a while, allowing my body to adjust as the other two worked me over.

I started riding him.

James reached around me and grabbed Nigel's hair and pulled him along my cock. He deep throated me as I did Jeffrey. His hands let go of Nigel's springs and touched my abs. His finger combed through my hair and circled my belly button. One digit entered and swirled around and around. He grasped my narrow waist and pulled me back, impaling me on his cock.

My cheeks spread as a warmth filled my ass. I felt him enter me inch by inch, opening me wider and wider as he went. I didn't think I could take any more, and he went deeper.

After all eleven inches were in, I felt his curly pubic bush scratch my ass. His cum filled balls slapped my cheeks and held me pinned in place. I moaned, and Jeffrey thrust deeper down my throat. Now, it was my turn to be spit roasted by these massive pieces of meat.

Nigel continued to lick my cock, as precum poured out of me.

James knew he could fit inside me, and he started to pull out of me.

My ass screamed, "NO!" as he withdrew.

As his mushroom head hit the ring, he thrust back in.

"Yes!"

James pulled me back onto his cock and bounced me against his pelvis.

I knew I was in for a wild ride.

Nigel backed up, unable to suck on my cock as James plowed me. He leaned back and thrust his pelvis forward, and I started to jack off his dick.

James' hand found my cock and wrapped around it. He stroked it as he humped my rump. Starting slowly, he quickly increased his speed in my ass and on my dick.

I knew this wouldn't take long.

Jeffrey stepped back and stood over Nigel's back, still jacking his cock. A fountain of cum flowed out of him and poured over Nigel's dark skin. As the load hit Nigel's face, he shot his load. Ropes of spunk sprayed out of him and hit my belly.

James slammed into me hard, and my whole body clamped down on him. I felt him buck against me as he entered me to the hilt one last time. He drilled deep into me and let out a great "Ahhh." His hand continued to work me using Nigel's hot spunk, and my balls exploded.

I watched as I frosted Nigel with glistening rows of thick cream.

James collapsed on top of me, pushing forward, so I landed on the cum-covered Nigel. His hot body caught mine, and we slid up and down each other. James' cock popped out of me, and he landed on the floor behind me. I felt his face land on my ass, and his tongue licked the bruised opening he had just exited.

We lay in a slippery heap.

Sam's gasped reminded us of the others, and we turned to watch their bodies climax on the table top. Spurts of cum sprayed in all directions across the table.

I felt our body fluids run down my torso and pool under my body.

James rimmed my butt and inserted his tongue. More cum spilled out of my dick and flowed onto Nigel.

Jeffrey rose and came back with a few paper towels. He handed one to each of us.

The rough paper scratched my sensitive skin as it tried to absorb the cum. The room smelled of men and sex. I let my body go limp and savor the moment.

One by one, each Spice Boy stood up and slowly started to dress.

I found my clothes and slipped on my underwear.

"WOW," Sam said from the table. He struggled to get to his feet.

I smiled. "I told you I was right." I stepped into my pants and zipped them up.

"We're going to make some beautiful music together," James said, as he winked at me, "and let's make it last forever, our friendship never ends."

A SWEAT, UNLOAD AND GOODBYE TYPE OF THING
By Derrick Della Giorgia

Hair style dictated by the pillow he'd not much earlier removed his face from. A dubiously clean white T-shirt. Sneakers worn without socks. In no way fat, but definitely overweight with meat to spare around his belly. Dark skin. That was the guy I was looking at. Honestly. Was I becoming a woman? That was the dream man of all my straight friends. Because he was sexy even if he wasn't perfect – like they claimed – or because anything more perfect than that – and it wasn't hard – fell under the category of "gay or otherwise known as unreachable" – as I was firmly convinced. That is up to you to decide. The disturbing news was that I really liked him. Seat next to the toilette – there, another sign of his pseudo-dirtiness? – on the Alta Velocità train that was taking me, too, to Florence, fingers glued to his Blackberry the whole time, he was distracting me from the science paper I was supposed to read before meeting professor Rossi.

No, I wasn't becoming a woman. I was simply acting like a straight man myself. I would never want him as my boyfriend – for that I needed clean, well groomed and sophisticated. I just wanted to blink at him, step into the toilet before the hour and a half train ride was over and fuck like an insect in that ridiculous little space. Just like a straight man wants the perfect woman to marry and a nasty fuck to spice life up.

He wasn't even hot. Two more lines into the protein synthesis experiment, I actually came to the conclusion he was short and borderline ugly. And I still wanted to fuck. I still wanted to weigh in my hand the bulge I couldn't take my surprised eyes off. I knew he noticed I was looking at him. He even got annoyed. Annoyed as in 'What the fuck are you looking at?' At that point, he couldn't imagine the absurdity of my demand. Perfectly wrapped in my suit, I certainly didn't give the idea of someone who wanted to get cock in his mouth. Annoyed as in 'What the fuck do you want?'

More Blackberry for him, more staring for me. Twenty minutes left before my cab ride to professor Rossi's University Department. Was it diversity I was looking for? Do we always want the opposite of what we have? Or do straight women really have it right when they pick the uncaring, basic model of Homo sapiens? *Trenitalia* cart squeezed through the seats, and he stopped the guy pushing it. Coffee and *La Gazzetta dello Sport*, the popular pink newspaper that no macho could do without on

Monday morning. While still using the phone to scratch his balls, my friend gulped down the espresso and disappeared behind the pink paper. Roma-Milan 2-1. Berlusconi doesn't comment.

The first page titles were of no interest to me. So I decided to give up on my fantasy and finish my work instead. The research project I was working on was my own idea. I finally had the chance to discuss it and sincerely hoped to get funds to sponsor it. My hormones could wait. On top of that, Pierpaolo didn't need to be cheated on again. I'd merely avoided losing him the last time that happened. Was it worth risking again? I guess there is no difference between a straight and a gay man when it comes to sex desire management.

"We are now arriving to Firenze Santa Maria Novella. We kindly request passengers not to open the doors before the train has completely stopped." This time taken by the western blot that was the main finding of the Australian colleagues, I hadn't realized I was already there. I unplugged my laptop and gathered all the shit I'd taken out of my bag, without forgetting my jacket on the overhead shelf. Now, I could see him again. He was yawning without covering his mouth. What a show – I thought before giving him the last hard look.

"Excuse me." He cut in front of me. His final destination was Florence, too. Leaning against the toilet door, he waited for the train to stop. In the limited space behind him, I confirmed my initial fear about his hygiene. He did emanate a vague sweat odor, that first warning of overheated armpits. To his defense instead, his arms were more muscular than I'd been able to see. His triceps dangerously approached my face when he pulled his jeans up.

The sucking noise of the door opening announced our time together was over, but I still believed it was a waste. An unjustifiable waste of good time, to depart from each other like that, without taking advantage of our miraculous compatibility: his wanting to get off and my wanting to let him do so in my mouth. In one of those moments that only natural selection can explain, I pushed my laptop bag into his ass. Why? I don't really have an answer to that question. It's like when you justly get a ticket and still try to convince the street police to let you go. You know there's no way, but why not try? At least that was the Italian way to see it. I would have been behind a desk in twenty minutes, he would have been out of my life in less than five. Why not try?

"Sorry!" I immediately specified when he slowly turned to me to see what was going on. With a simple nod, he put an end to the issue.

In the cab, I kept analyzing the anatomy of that perturbing attraction and my relationship with Pierpaolo. Uninterestingly, I didn't come to any conclusion that went beyond the simple concept that a rigid marriage is doomed to failure, unless one decides to accept sacrifice and invest his sexual energy into something else. Nothing against marriage, just skeptical of people's perseverance to deny that basic truth. Sex is like hunger, it doesn't last long once you quench it. Love, on the other hand, is much harder to explain with human physiology. It requires time and repetitive interaction.

Still with the change in my hand, I jumped out of the cab and hid into the toilet of the university bar. The picture of his body abandoned into the *Trenitalia* seat was stuck to my mind, stopping me from concentrating on anything else other than my hard-on. As accustomed to when Pierpaolo was out of reach, I yanked it out and started beating it. It felt good. I sucked on my left hand, dreaming of his dirty cock. I was sure he would have forced me to swallow, too. If only for the empowering pleasure of humiliating me. I would have been so into that, too. Nothing like spraying cum into the sink while checking your tie in the mirror!

With my balls alleviated, I proceeded into professor Rossi's studio to test my science. For a whole hour, I forgot about my train little adventure and managed to get amazing feedback on my research. Apparently, my idea was not completely new, but the methodology I'd confectioned seemed to be the only way to test that hypothesis, and the old professor gave me his word I would hear from him very soon. Elation invaded me as I stepped out of his room. A kind of corporal gratification slightly different than the toilet procedure but just as powerful! At 4:00 pm sharp, I was in front of my train again ready to return to Rome.

I am not the kind of person who believes in destiny. I would love to do that, together with many other kinds of comforting habits. But, I simply cannot. So just take what follows as you please.

Seated in the same car I was in, in my opinion slightly dirtier than in the morning, the same guy. A quick encounter – as life-altering as it can be – is wiped out of one's memory within 24 hours. A memory reinforcement like that becomes harder to get over. Back into my fantasy, back into the toilet sucking on his cock. Already riding my new hard-on, this time I happily met his girlfriend. He wasn't travelling with *La Gazzetta dello Sport*. He was with *piccola* and all the sweet kisses she was covering him with.

She kept teasing his neck with her glossed lips, but he wouldn't move an inch the hand that rested on her white skirt. He preferred to remain immobile until he could freely obtain what he wanted. Liking the same sex gives you an advantage. You can perfectly decipher those almost unnoticeable body reactions that speak louder than any words. His eyes were screaming for sex. Not sex as in long and affectionate exchange of love, but a quick and nameless fuck. A sweat, unload and goodbye type of thing. A nice and regenerating Friday night S.U.G. – as I'd baptized the practice.

Considering my results for the day had been accomplished and I still didn't have anything to lose, I bet everything on my sex-equals-hunger theory and did it. I elbowed him as I passed him and signaled with my head to follow me into the toilet. He didn't budge. He cautiously analyzed the situation, kissed *piccola* a long asphyxiating kiss, whispered something into her blonde fluffy hair. Ten seconds later, he locked the toilet door behind us and started working on his orgasm.

"Do you want to suck?" His low voice betrayed his fear of being caught. He extracted his cock while it wasn't yet completely hard and offered it to me. He didn't intend to do anything else, I supposed, but being sucked.

I didn't answer. I knelt in the room he created for me spreading his legs and took it into my impatient throat. When he was reassured I did want to suck, he became more creative than I would have accredited him. He wrapped my tie around his wrist, using it as a leash and pushed my head down with the other hand. Compromised by the train vibrations and his sex trap, my balance was extremely delicate, making my oral exercise more appetizing.

"Do you swallow?" Same tone, same fear. He was feeding his fantasy with the picture of his pleasure filling my submissive body. Penitent in my pagan miniature temple, I served the straight man in a way his sweet girlfriend couldn't probably do.

He got fully hard. Fully efficient in fucking my mouth. My head for that matter. I returned the favor allowing him to descend a little bit more into me.

"Swallow me!" This time, the excitement slipped through his lips. He extracted his Blackberry from his back pocket and started filming me. "Suck on it!" Something sweet dilated on my tongue; he closed his eyes; I prepared to swallow.

A BOY CAN DREAM, CAN'T HE?
By Francis A. Lewis

I'd told you of those dreams I started having mere months into our relationship. There was no need to worry. They weren't of the hopes and wishful-thinking kind. Those can be precipitous, no? Expectations are for fools. No, these were dreams of the nocturnal kind. The dreams I count sheep to get to. The ones I fall into spent but listless, after pulling at the heart strings between your legs, thinking of you. The ones I get trussed in a plush down comforter for. The ones I have to down a fifth of something amber against a clinking bed of ice for – so biting on its way down that dreams can creep up on me like dusk. The ones I have to wait for the darkest of dark for these days.

I am sitting almost upright against a wall with peeling white paint. There at the corners, it hangs, like dog-eared pages of a book you intend to return to. There's a panting gust coming from the small vent in the corner and its blowing at its edges. It could be the sound of lust seeping through, but it's probably just the hissing from something mechanical, maybe a furnace in the basement. I am on the first floor because it's easy to escape this way. The ceiling is but ten feet above my head even in this position. and I can see everything from this vantage point over my laptop's screen. It serves as some horizon, the only horizon because these frosted windows to the right of me are shut tight and though there are no curtains, only a sliver of light is peeking through. I haven't seen outside since you've left me. The florescent bulb hanging from an exposed wire on the ceiling is the sun or an undernourished-yet-illuminated baby dangling, its mother, its lifeline tucked away in the apartment above.

Just past my horizon, I can see an unused stove, its four ranges covered by a dusty microwave on top, because a stove in a place this small seems so cruel I can't bear to use it. Behind a bent black steel rod with a white sheet laying heavy on it, stands a porcelain toilet next to a claw-foot tub so close they seem one rather ingenious contraption. Think that's why I have taken to peeing in the shower lately, my faculties not belonging to me anymore, things like loose bowels so perfunctory these days. A waste bin next to that I use just for wads of tissue paper, cigarette butts snuffed at the root, and crumpled pieces of eggshell construction paper with pleading words worth throwing away. There's no sofa, there's no area rug because there's no true area to cover. Plus, there are floorboard planks that are covered in lacquer so thick I've taken to peeling some off with my fingernails when I have the time, when I can't stand the comfort of a bed and need grounding, when I am not so consumed with you.

All I can see now though, focus on, is wall paper peeking through these white walls. Like subcutaneous fat, past the epidermis, past the dermis, the white paint just thin layers of skin, shedding, peeling, letting go, being fought off. There are sanguine red flowers, the wall paper so beautiful, so stained with age, so resistant it's pushing off some cruel being's idea of what makes things modern. Someone thought of modernity even in this dump, yes. Why modernity equals all things white and metal these days? White walls, white furniture, white sheets and just metal appliances and accents and somehow you are current. It's war. Pale-faced subterranean pugilists with gunpowder on their fingertips, in their hair. But it's a losing battle. Minimalist they call it, I guess. It's more insane asylum if you ask me. It was the pugnacious flowers from the yesteryear wallpaper that brought and kept me here though, how they seem to have a fight still left in them.

I traded things, like luxury, like my obsessions, for this small clinical studio apartment in some high rise I know you will never visit. It once belonged to this color-blind artist who lived here, died here. He'd slept on this bed, probably sat against this very wall, contemplating things like this wall paper. He wouldn't have been able to distinguish the red rose from its green leaves and the very thought left me heart-broken.

I tried to prove throughout our whole relationship that I was just that: color blind. I tried to prove that I saw you only as someone I loved. But that's it, isn't it? Is love something to be proved? But how fitting I should be shacked up here in this artist's last abode to connect with the dead while you still live and breathe. Though his blindness was probably caused by some optic, retinal or acute brain damage, we are one in the same. He's my comrade, my confidant these days.

He painted with the fervor of a madman I could have only assumed. When I got here shortly after his parting, I'd studied his paintings still in their places, like a museum, me its curator of sorts. On their stark-white canvases, they were stretched so tightly on these small plywood contraptions that they seemed threadbare before their time. They were everywhere: strewn on the floor, leaning against the baseboards, on tables, on his bed, in the stove, in the tub. I didn't know how he slept or bathed, how he did anything really. Do you have to for the sake of art though? I write poems for you, my love. Keepsake odes with stanzas just long enough to render anyone speechless but you. I don't call it art, but I barely sleep, barely have the wherewithal to bathe in the hope these words will find you well, thinking of me – even if just a facet of a bygone era. I need anything to break the dead in this place. I can taste it on my tongue as of late. It's acrid and ... inviting.

When his parents came two weeks later to take his works and very little else, they told me about Michael (that's his name) as if he had been their everything, as if I'd known him, too. And I did know him, could tell that we thought of the world similarly. After they'd gathered up his paintings, they both looked about the place, saw how the light had left, and felt sorry enough for me to leave me with one. All of his paintings were black silhouettes, this one no different, like those inkblot tests they give to render one depressed, disturbed, or whatever. I think of those paintings, the one they gave me tucked under my bed for safe-keeping, as much as I think of you. I think of how they found his lifeless body at the foot of this very bed, tangled white sheets around his neck, as much as I think of you. The chatty landlord who rents me the place told me he'd had his paintbrush in hand, hardened dead fingers around it, mid-stroke perhaps. And I wondered if it had black paint still stuck on its bristles, if it found its way into the sheets. I kept everything his parents didn't take, including the bed, its mattress doused in something akin to bleach to mask the smell of death.

So it's here I sit, on this bed that isn't mine, slumped low now against a wall that isn't mine because it belongs to these roses, wilted and courageous as they are. And I am thinking of those dreams I started having mere months into our relationship – or, whatever you would now call it. Or worse yet, when the tides changed, and you had no words for what we were anymore. A liability? A mistake? Too varied? A reason to rethink, overanalyze, over-intellectualize things? And me? I never had the capacity for such cerebral things, not when it came to whatever we were. Love is too tangible for me. You see, you want it, you take it, you live it. But only if it's mutual. See, I wade in uncomplicated waters, while yours always seemed so turbid, muddied, everything so based on pragmatics, practicalities that to the laymen or the childlike it doesn't really exist.

So while I was living mindlessly in the blissful moments we shared, a wisp of a time it seemed before trouble set in and uprooted this mess, I'd do things like caress your cheek, taut and perhaps hesitant, with the back of my hand and hoped some of your luster – just the luster you exuded and not the color like you'd expect – would rub off on me, that I would somehow be more than the mere mortal I was.

No, I can't, I won't go there. It was these things, these envious thoughts, which may seem self-deprecating to some but ravenous to you, that brought us where we are today, you say. You'd look at me with stern eyes, eyes I hadn't seen before but would thereafter many times over, disapproving brown eyes, and say I exoticized things, that I exoticized you. Though still to this day, I am not sure if I truly know what that means. Do I think you exotic? Yes. Do I find your touch erotic, like that simple thing you started to do with your index finger against my bottom lip to silence me when we were in one of our small tiffs or the way you held me at the crook of my back with your left hand and the other intertwined with one of mine when we'd dance those dances in your bedroom for laughs, for our own variety of foreplay? Yes.

All I knew, just knew with all I was, was that I loved you for all the reasons you hadn't banked on, intended.

Still you say I had this unhealthy fascination with your physical. Though it seemed so practical to me that I would fall for someone taller than I, more serious than I, more potent than I, more grounded than I, more sinewy than I, darker than I, but only because you were all those things.

That defining question an hour into our first date of "have you ever dated someone Black before" took me off guard, was foreboding but relevant enough to you it seemed that I changed the subject. I didn't know the right answer, what would have made you bolt quicker. You held tight to the word "black" that night, your teeth seething the word, so I'd at first thought you meant if I'd ever dated someone sinister, with a black soul or heart. And I wanted to say "yes," I wanted to shout "yes." That's why I agreed to the blind date in the first place, why I'd put my love life in the hands of some woman, a work colleague no less, who'd known me for but a few months. Though she seemed my shaman, my spiritual advisor of sorts because she had the wherewithal to set us up, to bring me you, my angel of little mercy, I've come to find. But, I get the question now, probably even knew it then and, yes, you were the first, but would that have made a difference? Did you want to feel special, like you were the first, or did you want to be understood, like I could relate through empathy perhaps? I didn't know what it meant to don your skin, but I would, if you wanted me to, if I could have, I would. I would have let you flourish and wouldn't cover you up like this sterile white paint against my walls. I'd be the superhero for the day, week, month, year, eternity. Would that have made a difference?

That first night when you took me to your apartment, that formidable walk-up in Cobble Hill, that seemed a storefront rather than apartment complex, the one with the steel or

44

overwrought iron steps that led us up and would eventually bring us back down, you gave me that all-encompassing embrace at the entryway. It was refreshing after so many years of shoddy ones from others. It seemed we traveled to this outer crust of the Earth. Or was it just me? Was I the only one smelling something foreign, other-galaxy, and incongruous like junipers in the stifling air in that doorway? Or was it just your cologne that hung there among the exposed beams on the ceiling like a cloud taunting me? Or was it my, what did you call it, unctuous, yeah, my unctuous comments about your kind eyes that sprayed some fruit-like scent that first night? Whatever it was, I fell into your eyes, eventually into your arms, dizzy from it all and the helping embrace became more to me. Was that the moment where I knew I wanted to spend the rest of my life with you, and you knew I had what we now deem "issues." I saw heavenly bodies – yours and celestial things around that – that night and since then. I didn't want to resurface, to plummet back down. Was I the only one?

Did you always have reservations even as we packed my things from that East Village apartment my mom was paying for and willfully moved them to yours? It had been two months then and, if you had doubts, there must have been a blind eye you evoked. Though I can't imagine you not being self-aware, forethoughtful enough, to know if it wasn't right for you. Again, that same stairway, some passage way between past and future, was in plain view as we lugged my baggage up and down, planned to make a commitment I would never have backed down from. I climbed those icy stairs with no abandon. Did I just not see a misstep on your part, some dawdling in your gait? My boxes of personal effects, what could fit in boxes, were littering your bedroom, your kitchen, that living room with the smells, while my furniture, the big stuff, was in storage at your insistence. Was that some clue I missed? Why? Because you thought we wouldn't last, that this was inevitable? Was there a moment of contemplation I missed? Was there a moment before I clung to you, physically and metaphorically like dew to some flower, maybe a Black Pansy that you realized this wasn't going to work?

Still there was friendly fire at dinner that first night. I remember it all so vividly. And you got so comfortable so quick, or too comfortable too quick, my shyness easy to circumvent, had me all figured out. But I was still trying to feel things out, you see, wondering if you found me as attractive as I found you. The way you eyed me and walked and talked the unchartered first-date course of politics, astrological signs, religion, economics, socioeconomics was terrifying. But I found respite by focusing on, being mesmerized by the way you held your fork like some swordsman fighting your green peas. You were fighting off something back then, in the beginning, and I never assumed it could have been me. I was ok if it was the world, but I didn't want it to be me. We were in this together and the world I could battle, but I couldn't battle me anymore, I couldn't team up with you to fight me. I hadn't the wherewithal left for that.

It just couldn't have been me you were fighting. Not when afterwards, the cab let us both off. It could have sped off with me in it. After a dutiful walk around your block, where it seemed the true melting pot of New York lay with its factions of ethnicities, their restaurants, their haunts, so much of their everything that I felt drunk, you invited me back to your place. We could have stopped the hurt then. I would have died a painful yet recoverable death if we parted ways then, but we could have stopped the hurt in its tracks. But, there we were in your doorway, and in no time, I moved just a bit from your embrace, so I could lap at your erect nipples that favored ebony stones or missiles with these mystical powers. I didn't know where I'd gotten the courage. I couldn't resist those nipples though, and I went for them like I was a suckling baby, and you were taken aback at first but let things ensue for minutes. Your bright white tank was still on, and I had to maneuver around the straps that cupped your shoulders made of granite and your underarms that smelled like what I'd hoped I could soon characterize as your scent. I didn't mind; did you? When I let go, that stronghold I had on your left nipple released, I wasn't satiated but was overcome with thoughts of whether I was coming on too strong, coming off as some toppish freak ready to pounce when I truly just wanted you in me. I wanted to be your vessel. Did I ever tell you that?

I could see your nipples wet from my tongue or maybe from the summer's heat. I lunged for them again when I didn't see disgust or sadness or worry in your eyes, and then I went for your belt buckle a bit too early for you, and you took hold of that hand rabid and not belonging to me it seemed, looked me squarely in the eyes and whispered "let's take things slow." Your voice was deep and vibrating like a hum from a hive of bees. I crept up close to your mouth, kissed your chin gently, wanting to be stung, wanting the strong inflections of your voice to hit me like a ton of bricks. I pressed up against you, head to heart, knees slightly bent, deeper than before, thinking and knowing you could withstand me fully on you, feeling the dampness my saliva or the sun made on your shirt. I thought about what shapes we would make in your bed later that night, years to come, what oblong continuous circles we could produce, what colors we could create with our bodies. Hues of grey? Fitting as everything we'd become ended up being just that: nothing clear cut, nothing just the way it seemed. But I am ok with that. Do you read me? I am ok with that!

We kissed, and your tongue met mine, though rough to my soft. Your lips were cloud-like pillows though that stayed on the outskirts of mine, like you were sucking me in, breathing life into me. I tried to grab hold of one of them, the bottom one perhaps, so I could feel what suckling you would feel like at this angle, but, there you were again taking me in, your lips overthrowing mine, devouring every bit of me while we lingered up against a wall made of mortar and exposed brick. It felt like there was some turf war, that we were amidst some pitched battle. Should I have known then that there was a power struggle? If I'd known I would have surrendered, been your whatever, to lessen the blows and the questions today. But, maybe, that's it: I lacked a backbone strong enough to withstand all of this. But, to be honest, if we are to really be honest, I struggled before you and probably will after you with the inequities of my selfs. I pluralize that because, aren't we all just many different selfs walking around? One day we could be any combination. Over confident, creative, wildly attractive, family-oriented, self-sufficient, self-indulgent and the next day we aren't any of those?

But then I had to tell you about those dreams I started having mere months into our relationship. We were at some dive in Harlem that served what you said was the city's best calamari and impending poet and literary laureates. You said they were "bound to rule their respective worlds." And though I didn't know it, or maybe because I didn't, I coveted that world, like you probably knew I would. There in that place so cavernous and underground that dimmed lights seemed appropriate, the indigo light made you seem an X-ray, a transposed, one-dimensional copy of the man I once knew, or thought I knew. I said things I would take back now if I could. The whites of your eyes, those sparkling white teeth even seemed blue from the ambient lighting. I had to keep my right hand firmly on your left, thinking I was bound to lose you, that you would filter into the beckoning black wall behind us to nothing. I could feel something like tendons tensing up, pushing me away, but I kept my hand there, to stronghold you into place. You conceded but like those in the midst of giving up often do.

The lull of voices around us kept me there in reality, allowed me to say things I thought could never be said. So I told you of the dreams, not my hopes, but the dreams I started having mere months into our relationship. Those dreams so seemingly real, I had to tell you, whisper into your ear like sweet nothings. I am stark naked, walking along a concrete walkway in some garden with rows and rows upon rows of cotton plants and Summer Snowflake Viburnum on one side, the other teeming with Black Pansies. I walk halfway down the path, which seems to take years, though even in my dream I know it's only minutes, and something, some force, someone pushes me in the bed of pansies. I am rolling in them, picking and smelling them, uprooting and even eating some. I forget the other side, and I swim and swim. I am not naked anymore though as it seems with all the rummaging I inadvertently fashioned a loincloth of sorts with the pansies. I am happy. I am full. I am careless. I am full. I am free. I am full.

There, on my back in a sea of pansies, I see images pressed in the sky, silhouettes made from fluffy clouds of my mother, father, my two brothers, Granny, Pa, some past boyfriends, all huddled together in indistinguishable masses. They are like big blobs of cotton balls. I am the only one who can identify them, even in my dream I know I am the only one who could pick them up out of the sky's lineup. I am all knowing. I am free. I am full. Then I wake up.

You told me you'd been coming to the spot in Harlem "for years now," and I felt slighted, like you had some secret life that you didn't want me a part of. But, shit, I was there now. That had to mean something. And here I was telling you about a dream that I could have kept to myself. You patiently let me finish, well barely, and then slowly, effortlessly started talking, whispering in my ear as if endearments about indigo and cotton plantations, about the symphony of pain on the backs of your ancestors. There was a glint in your eye, the left one, that made me weary that I had sparked some unchartered nerve, or dimmed one perhaps. Then you explained that even the jeans and shirts we wear can be traced back to the backs of your people. I felt slighted again, like I didn't belong, like you led some secret life, but, shit I was there with you. That had to mean something. I listen intently, partly to appease, partly because I was shocked that that's what you gleaned from the meaning of my dream. I told you only because I thought you would be able to see past the cryptic and love me for who I am. But, then again, who was I that day? Who am I any day? Selfs just fighting selfs.

Something made you shudder, rethink things and you talked about how there was a difference between one who could sympathize and one could empathize. After a long day of work, you say, you needed someone who could empathize. "I am not blaming you," you said, pulling your hand discretely away considering the force. You were just looking forward as if entranced, and you wouldn't respond to my wanting to see those eyes falling, moving farther and farther from my view. "Sure, you are missing a few pieces," you'd said, your peripheral only showing, "but you are a great person. I just really need to think about things, really think things out."

When the waiter, just a shadow of a black button-down and white-turned-purple pants walked over with our calamari dipped in darkness, I looked past him and saw these literary geniuses you raved about for the first time as if they appeared from nowhere, through some dream sequences perhaps. They'd seemed to morph into life forms from the sky, the ceiling, maybe some secret passage way. Surrounding some 4x4 stage, they sat waiting their turn, in these flimsy chairs that had to have been swiped from some patio setup. These men of rich backgrounds, like Senegalese, like Puerto Rican, like Jamaican, like Ecuadorian, like Harlemites, like Brookynites could rule the world with iron fists attached to their arms veined, muscular, tense like yours, and I wouldn't have any objections. I wanted to be a part of that world, wanted to belong, be yours, be there, with you, with these beautiful men, seeming anachronous, Harlem-Renaissance-like, wading, waiting to go on stage for their turn to scream jagged metaphors and piercing similes. What I could see of their eyes seemed so pained I wanted to quit my job right then and there, parlay a career into anything, anything other than investment banking, tell my mom her prodigal son had no use for the trust fund that would mature when I was twenty-five, forfeit the degree I landed from some school others would laud but not worth mentioning, where three generations of the Conroy Family languidly roamed its hallowed halls and supplant everything for pain, burden, the need for redemption. You want empathy? There it is!

The Poets were still camping out on the sidelines. Poet Number 1 whispered to Poet Number 2 about something funny enough that they hang in languor, ghosted touching of hands, cupping backs, nuzzling ears. I want in on the whisper with my own secrets to share. Poet Number 3 is now on stage evoking the spirits of Hughs, Baldwin, and Ellison it seemed. He's unaware of the enchantment, the spells he casts with his words, or the magic between his cohorts on stage right. But I am there, some kindred spirit in the audience, desperately wanting to empathize.

But, you are right, I could truly only ever sympathize what with my pasty white skin, my irises bluer than most, my head start, my stead, the little tiny blond hairs on my arms so faint it looks as if I have none at all, my hands un-calloused, shadow of a man's hand, the way I could walk in a store and not be followed though my heart would pulse with excitement with just the thought.

It has always been your conviction that made me drunk though, want to drink you all in. Venerable – you have always been. But you didn't seem to care anymore, your mind made up. I was a flat, ripple-less as a pond in your eyes. But you are this listless, turbid rapid; I want to ride, brave the waves. That night you did slip away. The events thereafter I forget like they never truly happened. It's easiest that way. All I wanted was to give you my truth: that I loved you more than I even loved myself. Why wasn't that enough?

... But maybe I haven't truly given you the whole truth about me, about how many pieces I am actually missing. Maybe I have lied to you because this studio apartment I sit in is but a room, with a door that has the tiniest window imaginable (not for my sake but for the staff who periodically looks in on me). It looks out onto corridors with other rooms just like it. And maybe, I am not allowed to have a computer in these confines. My toes and nail beds are so stark white from a lack of circulation from being strapped tight in this papoose of white sheets and worn leather straps that they look like a huddled mass of tiny clouds. Maybe that's my true horizon.

Yes, maybe, a color-blind artist lived here though I never met his parents, never had the opportunity to see his paintings. But I can dream, no? And that landlord is but a man, who dons white uniform, a tag with his name pinned to its breast pocket, who comes in from time to time to give me a worried look, a quick change perhaps for there is no bathroom in this room, and prescription drugs in these tiny paper cups to quell my fears, my anxiety over you. Maybe it does cost an arm and a leg to stay here, but my mom, she's fitting the bill as I can't work anymore.

And, maybe, just maybe I am not propped against a wall because that's hard when you are tied to a bed like I am. And maybe, just maybe, I do spend some time looking for the things my predecessor used to render himself lifeless at the foot of this very bed. Maybe it was nurture and definitely not nature that brought him to that decision, to the conclusion that life wasn't worth living anymore. I am fighting these thoughts though, hoping that this all will find you well and that you are in love with your counterpart, that person who makes you feel whole.

Or maybe we shouldn't find people who outfit us with their halves. Maybe we are all competing with selfs and should just contend with that. But if you are by your lonesome, I hope you are fighting off the peeling paint with your neon-colored flowers, with hues of the most electric red and greens. I hope you continue to be stronger than I will ever be, with your convictions and your laundry list of requests that I could never meet. I don't shame you for them. I pity me for not having some myself.

A boy can dream though. Though these, these are of the wishful-thinking kind. See me out of this haze, dreams. See me out of this haze.

BOYZ
By R. Talent

I think it can be agreed upon that both Tavarres and I went much further than we should have, given our fragile situation. We were boyz for Christ Sakes! We had been boyz since we learned to holler back at each other from our wooden prisons, or at least since we were pupils at Mrs. WandaMamma Preschool and Daycare Center. We went to school together, fighting over girls and sharing identical report cards. We even graduated together. Not like we graduated on the same day, but like he was literally right behind me when I went to grab my diploma because he was right there grabbing his. We even followed each other to the same historically black college and hooked up with a set of twins that was actually part of a set of fraternal triplets. Because our girls were girlz, and we were boyz, we all thought it would be cost-effectively fly to have a double wedding and be each other's best man.

There was hardly a time we weren't on the same page. Well, there was that brief moment in time when we considered pledging for different fraternities. Thankfully, I got him to see that if a man can't be the Alpha of the tribe, he might as well Omega his butt back home.

We definitely had our good times, but we also went through our bad times together, too, seeing each other through just about everything. I let him crawl under the sheets with me when I found out that he was dumb enough to still believe in monsters. I hopped into bed with him when the loud thunderous clap of lightening scared the bejesus out of me. When his mom got laid off from her factory job and their cupboards were bare, we broke bread like we were brothers tossing peas at each other's head. When it was a hard go at home, between my dad and stepmom, Tavarres just let me sit up in his room and play video games for hours on end, letting me be and working through the divorce on my own. I squeezed his hand at the gravesite when his baby sister lost her battle to Leukemia. And he let me sob like a baby in the back of his raggedy old Crown Victoria, when just the day before I was getting ready to meet my mom for the first time in my life she lost her life out there in the streets.

Even after we got through all that, we still ended up shedding a few more tears together. First, when we found out that we were swindled out of our life savings through a faulty business deal, and again, later on that day when we found out that the duplex we were renting was robbed. If that wasn't enough, after Tavarres and I started up a successful landscaping business, my wife had the nerve to take part of my fortune in the divorce only for it to come out that his wife, my ex sister-in-law, was cheating on him with a washed-up basketball player stunting out the last of his NBA contract money.

I wasn't worried about him, though. We both could've done better than we did, but looking back on it, we were so caught up in being brothers through marriage that none of the other stuff really mattered. So, as his best friend and former brother-in-law, I wasn't the least bit surprised that after his divorce proceedings went through that, Tavarres snagged him up a model on his way out of the courthouse, unlike me who made it rain with some of my rap connections at the local strip club.

No homo, but speaking straight up on the real, the real reason I wasn't worried about him was because my boy Tavarres is nothing more than a doe-eyed pretty boy with this long curly hair that the ladies all seem to go goo-goo gaga over against his very bright and shiny fair skin. Add to that being a hopeless romantic, I should've known that only he could turn a rebound into a second marriage. I tried talking some sense into him without crossing boundaries, but after he assured me that he got her to sign to a prenup, I was good.

I felt as if he upgraded for the both us when he married Carolyn on the shores of Hawaii. But I would be lying if I said I wasn't blown out of the water when he mentioned precariously that he was still warming up to the open marriage thing when he took the number of some flirtatious waitress who seemed turned on by his new wedding ring. He wasn't ecstatic about sharing his new bride with other men, but being that she was so generous about offering up some of her phyne model friends, he wasn't boohooing too badly. Especially the way she seemed to get off on him getting off. And with him giving her a short list of men to get it on with (which ironically most of them were high-profile athletes), he mocked that at least he knew what his wife was up to this time.

He spent months trying to convince me that everything was okay in his world. That he was having the time of his life screwing all these magazine girls. He might've fooled everyone else with his bragging, but all I had to do was look into his eyes and see that there was a sad story behind him. This was especially true when he spent those quiet nights laid out on my couch, acting like he hadn't a house to go home to. I guess those nights were catered to her and her lovers, which he was *glad* to point out whenever they made it on the television for one thing or another.

Then one day, out of the clear blue, he showed up on my doorstep with the cheesiest grin plastered across his face, telling me that his wife wanted to be with a regular guy. That she wanted to have a threesome with the both of us. I could see that he was a little hurt that I wasn't nearly as excited about the proposition as he was, given that we were boyz and all. I guess my thing was that while he had a hot wife, she was still his wife. We fought over the same girl, not fucked them.

After a few weeks, after they assured me that they were totally cool with the whole thing, I eventually got used to the idea, too. On one end, I was kicking myself that the two of us didn't about doing anything like this back in college. So rather than marrying a couple of tramps, we could've had a real bonding experience in a foursome with our twins. On the other end, I was a little bit curious of where Carolyn would rank me amongst her athletic conquests.

As rightfully suggested, before the three of us even entertained the idea of a threesome, Carolyn and I needed our own time as man and woman. I thought I was going to be able to get it in and get it off the first time around, simply because I was a man that was weak for nookie. But the mental block came down on me hard the second we climbed out of our clothes. Even with Tavarres' blessing, it still felt wrong. This was still his wife. Maybe it was because I was standing right there with her when my boy decided to dedicate his life to her. After a few flings, though, over here and over there, I started to feel like my piece was putting claims on that red snapper.

The night came, and I just *happened* to walk in on the two of them making out in their bedroom. I came up behind her, and we got to it. The three of had a great time, but I think Tavarres and I were surprised how naturally things came to us. Not that we fucked or anything like that, because it stayed mostly about his wife, but it sort of spooked us the way we were looking at each other from time to time like we were the only ones in the room. The electricity we felt when we reached out and touched the other's dicks. The comfort we felt rubbing our hairy balls together taking care of two neighboring holes. What I won't ever forget was when his wife was in my lap, riding it out like a champ, and he standing in front of me feeding her his bone with his round ass in front of me that I couldn't fight the urge of nuzzling my face between his honey-glazed cheeks.

I didn't eat him out. I just breathed warm air over his hole that caused him to heave, leaving Carolyn to believe that she had upped her game.

I think we both knew we crossed some kind of ethical line, when I came between her legs and he came in her mouth only for the both of us to enjoy the sloppy seconds of the other, enjoying the warmth and goo left there by the other.

We probably spent the next couple of hours after that dozing in and out of catnaps, looking past his snoring wife at the other playing sleep, pretending that we didn't share some kind of connection when we snuck off downstairs to raid the refrigerator.

"You don't think Carolyn would mind us leaving her like that?" I asked with the innocence of a two-year-old boy.

"The way we put her lights out, she'll be down 'til morning." He said grabbing both a creamy light-colored pie and some protein shakes.

We started eating some of the pie. And because we were sitting across from each other for the first time without the sex, for me it was like I was looking at him in a whole different light. It wasn't like I wanted to do him then and there as much as it was the settling of seeing my boy naked, which after all that we went through flustered me with a slight embarrassment.

It wasn't like I had never seen him naked before. Mostly just in his underwear, with the rare occasion of catching him passing through on his way from the showers and the locker room. Oh, I nearly forgot about the time we came across my brother's *Gents* magazine, and we had a jack-off competition to see who could beat off the fastest to the morose-looking white girl with the Double Ds. The last one to bust off was gay. So we weren't looking per se, as we simply caught fleeting glimpses. Well, at least, that all it was for me.

"So are we going to talk about it?" Tavarres asked, forking his side of the half-eaten whipped razzleberry pie with the chocolate crust.

"Only if you want to," I said eating my half of the pie, noticing his greasy legs sneaking out of his partially opened robe. "This has more bearing on you than it does me."

"Oh, really," he said modestly. "Because if I recall you were the one pressing your face between my cheeks."

"That's because it was winking at me, and as shapely as it was, I thought it belonged on some big booty chick."

"So I'm a bitch now. Alright," he said coolly.

"I didn't say all that. You're my boy … for life."

"Oh, no doubt," he laughed prematurely. "Back around the old neighborhood, nothing said boyz being down like blowing warm air up the asshole!"

"Fuck you," I chuckled.

"Seriously though, speaking as boyz," he said, choosing his words cautiously. "You're going to tell me that you never thought about me like that?"

"Man, c'mon, now," I said, dropping my fork in the aluminum pie pan.

"Let me finish. I'm not talking on some gay shit. I'm talking about as long as we've been there for each other. Have you ever felt torn between your boy and your wife?"

"You?" I threw back at him, devoid of the question he asked me.

Tavarres paused. "I'm not even going to lie. There've been times throughout both of my marriages that I preferred hanging out with you on your couch playing video games than coming home to either Juliet or Carolyn. Sex with my girl or hanging out with my boy, you figure out that logic."

"Wow," I said, getting the wind knocked out of me with a lot of truths coming at me at once. "So, in other words, while I've been thinking we're cool, simply as boyz, you've been secretly waiting in the wings for something more to become of it?"

"No."

"What do you mean no? You're sitting there telling me that after being married to two women you'd rather be with me."

"No, not the way you make it sound."

"How am I making it sound?"

"You're sort of putting off as if our friendship has been a lie, when in fact it's because of the love of our friendship that I haven't dared cross that line."

"Until tonight, you mean?"

"Never," he said sternly. "We've got nearly thirty years of friendship under our belts without anything popping off. What I'm saying is that I can go thirty more without it, as long as I know we're good."

"You're talking a lot of back and forth. On one hand, you're talking about our friendship being the most important thing, and then on the other hand you've invite me to your house to have sex with your wife? C'mon, now. Something ain't adding up."

"Look, as for that thing upstairs, I thought since it'd been a minute since you mentioned a girlfriend and my wife's a nympho that it'd be a perfect fit. If she's going to have sex with another man that's not me, I would prefer that she has it with a man that I love like a brother."

"I don't know, man."

"What's there to know? I'm not asking you to be my man or anything. I just think we got to acknowledge that something more happened up those stairs, other than the two of us DP-ing my wife."

"I don't have to acknowledge nothing." I said nervously.

"Like I said, we've been friend for almost thirty years now, I know you inside and out, better than anybody you can think of, so I know when something is stewing in your mind. So you're going to tell me that in all the years that we've known each other that you never once thought about me like that? Remember, there've been a number of days I've woke up to your 'morning sunshine' hammering at leg."

He was right. There was that one time that I was laying up in bed jacked off thinking about some girl had a crush on when at the last minute his shiny, freshly-washed caramel cakes came into mind.

"Okay, I can see by the look on your face you've thought about it at least once. So I'll break the ice and tell you that I thought about you in that way about three or four times."

"Three or four times?"

"Yeah," Tavarres said casually. "The first two times was totally by accident, though, both apart of this continuing dream back when we were playing football. It wasn't anything sexual. It was just one of those things that made me take note with a brick against the bed. The third time was the night of junior prom when you struck out with Chantella Strong, and you looked so freaking sad. Whether it was anything sexual to it, all I knew was that I wanted you to be happy. Even if I hadn't a clue about how to go about it. It wasn't until we were in line and some of the brothers got that queen from down the street to suck all of us off that I mildly got a clue."

"Huh? You mean that was a guy that sucked us off while we were blindfolded?"

"Yep," Tavarres laughed. "Now I know a lot of girls that will part their legs like the Red Sea for nothing, but how many women do you know will give thirty guys a blowjob at random."

"I thought we were blindfolded to protect their identity! And how do you know that was a guy?"

"Guys," he corrected. "It was like one to every three pledges. I didn't get the sleep mask-like blindfold, remember? I got a bandana tied over my eyes, and not very good since I could see right under it."

"Wow. Obviously, since you seem to know about my first time with a guy, what about you? Have you ever messed with another guy before?

"You mean other than rubbing poles with my best friend just a couple of hours ago? Yeah. But it was only that one time, back in high school when I had a two-week fling with Coach Henry."

"Coach Henry?!" I said shocked, thinking about the mean middle-aged man that nearly made me take a dump in my pants with his gargantuan size and ugly snarl.

"Yeah, but after the first week, I wasn't really feeling him like that, though. Not like I was into it like that, you know. I guess I started having feelings about you and not knowing what to make of them. He was there, I was there – let's just say that in the end I got into something real deep real fast, and when he started to become controlling with it, I had to find a way to climb out of it."

I looked at my friend again, for about the second or third time that night. Unlike before where it was something magical between us, this time it just felt like I was seeing him for the first time.

"So even if I did admit to feeling something up there, you might be against going down that road?"

"Yeah," he said, "but not because I'm not interested. I would be lying if I said I wasn't interest. But I can't see throwing away thirty years of brotherhood away on a nutt."

"Two," I joked, referring to the action that had recently transpired.

"Well, that really doesn't count, though. I knew full well what was I was doing when I suggested that she share herself with my boy. You can bang her every day from here on out, and it wouldn't change anything. Get her knocked up, I don't mind raising your seed. That's how much love I have for you. But to risk losing you from my life because we share something we may not be able to recover from would be too much for me to bear on my soul. So I can't even go there."

I let his words sink in, and I looked at him as I looked at him upstairs, unable to deny the energy that was surging through us. The energy that I had suspected that had always been there, but I was too stupid to see. Even when I found out my wife was a whore, that didn't nearly hurt me as much as when he told me that he was marrying Carolyn, as I had already made plans for him to live in my house for another year long, if not more.

"Come here," I commanded standing up.

"Why?"

"Come here, boy."

Tavarres was slow to his feet but got to them just the same.

Tavarres was far from fat. He did have a little meat on his bones that seemed to be more distinct than it should've been the way his pointy nipples slightly hung over his soft fleshy but flat belly.

Tavarres stood in front of me. I just looked at him look at me, and as if something else was just taking over, I put my lips tenderly over his.

I was so amazed at the effortlessness of our kiss that I hadn't a clue of how long it actually lasted. Second, probably minutes, had passed before we broke apart. We were left breathless after that, not by the motion as it was emotional connection.

"You can't be doing that," Tavarres huffed.

"We boyz aren't we?" I quickly answered.

The first time between us it was just a poignant kiss, but the second time it was laced with much more passion and heat, pulling him close to me by his exposed waistline as if he was rightfully mine, feeling his naked body through his open robe pressed against my silk boxers – the only thing I had on.

Ours tongues were wrestling, our bodies, longing. He was pinching my nipples like he's known forever that that was my spot. And in return, I put his face in my hands just like I somehow knew he needed that from me, too. He was hard. I was getting there, but I wanted him just the same. I don't know what I want to do, though. My body was screaming yes, and my heart was singing in accord. Being with his wife wasn't the same as being with him, I thought through. My head, my head kept on reminding me that there was a morning after to this, so I didn't want to go into this hastily. I wasn't sure if we were going to recover from me sleeping with his wife in front of him, and now if I went through with this that meant I would have to share my boy with his wife.

I had him on the large round sturdy table, leaning into him until we fell on it. His legs were wrapped my back, his hands caressing the top of my upper back. Thank God he had enough sense to buy quality furniture. It was more than kissing for me. I wanted to taste him, be inside him. The way he palmed my chest, making a flimsy plea to push me away felt oddly right wanting to save our friendship. But my milk chocolate banana stuffed in his crack felt even better, particularly the way the top skin of my hard dry dick felt against something so moist and ready just for me.

"We can't." Tavarres exhaled, but his hands roaming my back told another story.

"Yes, we can." I smooch his neck.

"My wife," he panted.

"Not anymore," I commanded. My hand somehow made its way down to his knee, and I felt the small scar left there by a steel rod from when he fell from atop Mr. Livingston's junk pile. "She wasn't there when you got that scar, and she has never been – ever. Not like I have. Not like I'm going to be. And if we're going to be honest, it'll kill me if I got to share you with anybody else. Let's not waste anymore time making the same mistakes as before."

"You're words are sweet," he said with my face on the other side of his neck and his dick throbbing between our stomach sandwich, "but, let me get this straight, you're saying leave my wife?"

I pulled up, just upright enough to look him in his eyes. "Don't just leave, divorce her, leave her with her athletes and make a clean break for it."

"What about the house, the cars?"

"You of all people should know best that I got you. Leave her with whatever she wants … except this table. It's going to become real special for the both of us in a minute. Maybe it's time to face fact that we put up with so much from these women because in the end nothing else matters in this world but you and me."

He looked up at me, he wanted to say something, but his mouth was trembling, and water was filling his eyes.

"What's the matter, babe?"

"I've been waiting a long time to hear those words, but as I listen to them, I can't help but wonder if we do what we do on this table how much it'll effect what we already have. Not only that, are you ready for the world to know about us like that?"

"Fuck the world! Don't you know I love you?"

He suddenly let out an incoherent moan.

I brought myself to find out what was going on, just to find out that the tip of my dick was already wedged inside of him. I guess getting upright to look into his eyes made for perfect alignment.

"We've been through hell and back for me to let you fall in despair now," I said, trying to easily ease up out of him, surprised that I got more than just the tip in.

He reached into his robe, pulled out some lube and handed it to me. As I smeared it on my dick and the outside of his hole, he came out of the armholes of his robe, allowing me to feel all of him against me.

I reached further down his body and grabbed his ankles. I'm not much of a man for paying close attention to things, but there was no way to deny that my boy had some pretty feet. All I could think about was cupping them in my hand as I worked my way into his shimmying ass.

I heard him wince as I pushed in, feeling his strict hole quiver around me. I wanted to ask was he okay, but his eyes told me his story. He was just fine as long as I was there, going slow and tender. I knew this for certain when I felt the hard ring of muscle up there deliberately give way.

His ankles fell from my hand and kept parallel to my back, wrapping his arms back around my back, letting me know that he wanted every bit of me inside of him. I let him know that I wanted the same thing, taking good care to be careful with my best friend, my boy.

As I was going deep in him, it was like everything we had ever been through in our lives had led us up to this point. So it was almost a mental shock that was so in tuned emotionally to him than I was mentally. Then it hit me: This wasn't just some fuck. Obviously, I knew that on some major level, but on another I wasn't sure what to expect it to be. Then it became clear that this was untainted lovemaking on a level that I had never experienced before.

I knew he had to have been feeling the same thing, the way he looked up with a teary-eyed smile and the way his hole just opened up for me, like it had been waiting a long time for my arrival. His insides opened wider than wide, and for some daggone reason, it decided to close shop on my dick. It took me a minute to comprehend that he was just trying to make it good to me, take care of me in his way.

I want to do the same.

I rocked my hips harder into him, and the moans that he was able to keep behind his lips seeped through his teeth, in low gasps with his eyes amazingly tight. Even though this was a first for me, I knew he was feeling more than that. I was feeling more than that, and I was on the other end, plus the realization that I was in my boy like that. So intimate, so free. He had me paranoid for a second. Then I slowed down enough for him to open his eyes up, and I saw that that was just as important to him as it was for me, but there was a huge weight of fear roaming bouncing behind the back of his head.

"I got you, Tavarres." I grunted, putting my name back on it. "You got to believe that. That's on everything I love, which you know is you. Just let it out, babe. Let it out! Let her hear you. Let the neighbors hear you. I don't give a shit! Even after this, they going to know we're together forever ... and ever ... and ever-ever."

I balanced my weight on my hands. I saw that he was fighting letting go of his inhibitions, but the prodding I was doing inside of him, even he had to give up his guard.

He was in the throws of the pleasure of it all, and I was relieved, glad that my best friend was letting me know how I was making him feel but quickly became mindful that we was on the still table. And the more he let go of his insecurities the less secure I felt about the table.

I picked Tavarres up off the table, never losing my place inside of him. His sweaty hands locked around my neck as I carried him into his den where he had a recliner, a chair I felt good about supporting us comfortably. As I sat down, I quickly realized that the position before felt primal, but this felt totally intimate, totally right.

"Yes! Oh, God, yes," he murmured, he just couldn't seem to control himself, grinding against me as I sucked on his nipples.

There was so much I wanted to do in that moment that I couldn't get where I wanted to be. My hands wanted his rump, to bounce him on my lap. He was most definitely hard, drooling with precum and straining for my undivided attention.

"No," he hissed, as I grabbed his dick, stroking it as I bounced him. "No."

My hands were in a perfect place, one supporting his backside and another milking his long slender piss rod, coming down just right on his family jewels.

Tavarres was gritting his teeth; moaning and groaning his way through tremors that had manifested itself into liquid fire that just shot out of his body and onto my chest and abdomen.

I couldn't stop after that. I just wouldn't. I needed to be inside even more, more urgently. I needed his body to respond to me and the affectionate whimpers that were making their way into my ear.

"Don't stop. Don't stop. Don't stop." He cried over and over again, shooting some more onto me just a second later and then continued on with his ramblings.

Just like he requested, I didn't stop. I bounced him on my lap, enjoying the best sex I ever had, kissing him and caressing him and looking deep into his eyes to reveal that this secret fantasy.

"Damn, baby, I need you to come," Tavarres breathed between kisses.

"I'm about to baby. I'm about to," was the most I could get out of my mouth, without losing my breath.

"Put your hands to your sides." He told me after some time.

I did, letting my hands fall over the other side of the armrests.

Tavarres just seemed to get into his zone and just started bucking me like I was his personal fuck toy. I tried getting a grip on him, but he just pushed my hands away.

"Just ride the feeling, babe. Just ride the fuckin' feeling."

So I did, and the way he was rolling on me, it was going to be hard to ride the feeling without losing it very soon. I heaved and hoed, my eyes wide shut just enjoying this, my best friend.

I kept on edging the point of no return just to come back. I wanted to solidify our bond by emptying everything I had inside of him. But, there was this other part of me that didn't want to end, not knowing what was going to become of us after this.

"Look at me," he said softly. "Look at me, you told me we we're good. Thirty years, thirty years more."

I looked into his eyes, letting him buck me like he had been. I felt his hole fluttering against me, before bolting down in all the right places. The sensation was great, but the comfort of looking into his eyes and knowing that we were going to good after that was simply too much.

"Oh, Goddamn!"

I grew stiffer, my dick went deep in his ass, and I felt every load I ever shot just jet out of me and into him.

I wanted to lie on top of him, but there was nowhere for us to do that, so the next best thing was for him to come down on me and welcome daybreak with our everlasting kisses.

Later on, in that space of morning of ending darkness and the beginning of the sun's light, when we went back upstairs, I think we were both spoofed to find Carolyn sound asleep in her bed after all those noises we must have made.

I wish I could say that he went upstairs, grabbed his stuff and drafted her a "Dear Jane" letter, letting her know that he was coming home with me. That was how I played it off in my mind of how it was going to go down in those final seconds before I came. But I had to become a bit more patient than that. I had to let him be a man about cleaning up the mess he made with his wife. I could be logical like that because, in the meantime, it wasn't a bad consolation prize that he spent every night after that with me at my house in my bed, fucking and making serious plans for our future.

I guess I could be cool like that because I couldn't wait to be his man when we spent the last thirty years being boyz.

SOLDIER BOY
By R. Talent

"Yo, you fuck it like pussy, right?"

Although I utterly despise the comparison of ass to pussy, knowing firsthand that both have two entirely different grips, I let out a boyish giggle unbecoming of the man I was, in the dark, streetlamp-lit room with this heavily-proportioned green-eyed soldier working his way between my knobby knees.

The day ended far different from what I expected; though, oddly enough it started and ended pretty much the same with me getting off another soldier from Fort McPherson before I was soon to send another one off into the abyss.

My day started off about a quarter to five after the alarm on my wrist buzzed me awake. It was important that I didn't oversleep. It was my goal to wake up my then-boyfriend of three months with another blowjob in our motel room. It wasn't that I was all that crazy about Montego or his crooked foreskin dick that I willfully swallowed his pineapple-flavored load, as it was my heavy conscious possibly giving him the last piece of memorable sex before he was to report to the base and possibly go off to war.

After I eased his trouser salute with a proper send off, I took to some mouthwash while he jumped into the shower as a civilian one last time and emerged as a formidable soldier in his fatigues. He was many hours away from reporting to base. But considering that he wanted his last meal as a free man to be at IHOP and we being limited to catch the bus to get around town, we broke off from our weekly stay, caught the bus, the train, and another bus to breakfast, and arrived at the train station outside of Fort McPherson with forty-five minutes to spare.

Because we properly said our goodbye back in the motel room like two freakishly gay men could, I simply walked Montego to the end of the sidewalk on the side of the train station and turned back around after I saw him safely cross the street and go through the gates.

Now, I will be the first to admit that even after all the motel-hopping Montego and I did before he went his way and I was due to go mine before I got medical clearance to get back on my eighteen-wheeler, I didn't have any strong emotional ties to Montego other than as a roommate and as a serviceman. But even I was floored over how easy I got over what's-his-face after I caught a glimpse of the strong broad back of this new soldier walking just feet in front of me back toward the train station. Even through his heavy fatigues, I could see that he had an incredible body to boot. Because I was a good little ways behind him, I didn't want to run out in front of him like some uncouth scumsucker to see if his looks matched his god-like aura.

"Men just look good in uniform," I reasoned through the budding crowd getting off a number of buses that pulled into the terminal, as I tried my best to hide the budding erection thudding down my pants leg.

Although I was open with my dealings with other men, I felt my uncontrollable actions were ridiculous for a man my age. Never in my life had I ever been so hungry for a man, seen or unseen. But this man had me, a couple of other men, and just about every other woman within twenty feet going the way his big muscled butt filled out those camouflage pants with every long Clydesdales stride he took in those camel-colored boots.

I honestly took no shame in enjoying the show going on before my very eyes as he made his way up the stairs, over the opened skywalk, through the fare gate, and back down the stairs to the awaiting platform. I was just a hair off from seeing his handsome face when his cell phone rang, and he darted off to the far end of the platform.

I played it coy, standing near the edge of the crowd to listen from a distance to his conversation. It was obvious from the initial pleasantries that were in his voice that he was talking to someone close to his heart, offering names and pet names in the most affectionate way that only a heterosexual man in love could. After that gushy display of affection, I started not to bother to even give him a second look (or take a mental image of him to jack off to later) when he just came out of nowhere exploded with venomous anger, calling the woman a low-down filthy whore and that she should've had her ass at the train station, waiting and ready to pick him up by now. Whoever was on the other end of the line was crying with apologies with him doing the same a few moments later. He listened for a minute more and kept on repeating through the phone that he would figure something out before hanging up on her.

"Damn," he burst, almost losing his cell phone in the train tracks below, as he threw air punches and kicks. "That damn bitch knew she had to pick me up, so I can get back home to my kids! Damn!"

He must've felt the many pairs of eyes descend upon him and quickly calmed down considering that he was still in uniform and could still be reported for his unprofessional behavior. He stood still for a minute more, patiently waiting for the stares to die down. And after enough pairs of eyes went about their business, he quickly started pacing a portion of the platform, wordlessly venting his anger. Mind you, I still hadn't gotten a really good look at this guy at this point, but the closer in he got before doing a full turnabout in the other direction, the more impressed I was with him and his comely looks. But then as he came in a bit closer, my heart completely sank.

He was an incredibly gorgeous black man, honey-colored skin with a clean shaven face that celebrated his rigid jaw line, and the softest green eyes ever found on a human being. But, as fate would have it, he was incredibly young for my selective taste.

At a glance, because of his bulky size, he looked to be about a doable twenty-five or so. Upon further inspection, however, his baby face suggested that he was actually a couple of years younger than that, which would've made him about six years younger than I was. If I was in the market for a muscle boy bottom to bang, he would've been right up my alley. No problem. But the way I made this soldier out to be in my head, more of a he-man than a mere boy, I was looking forward to putting my legs up in the air and getting my hole done right. That's not to say that either was going to happen, but for the sake of argument

I usually preferred my tops to be a tad older than I, as if they were mature enough to put a hurting on this grown ass.

As I boarded the train with my dreams dashed, I sat across from Soldier Boy just a few feet away. He tried to stay stoic in his express but couldn't fight back the tears swelling in his eyes.

While I had long given up on him being a noteworthy notch in my belt, there was something inside of me that wanted to reach out to this marred young man on a more affable level. I sat their nervously across from him trying to come up with a game plan to approach him. As station after station passed us by, and he steadily sat there with his face in his palms, I slowly walked over to the empty seat in front of him.

"Hey," I said, throwing up a deuce sign.

"Hey," he mouthed, more at a loss for words.

"Not to get into your business or anything, man, but I got on with you at the train station back there and saw your blowup back there. Is everything alright?"

I was looking for Soldier Boy to tell me to fuck off, that he was just fine and that he didn't need me in his business. Instead, he was very forthcoming about his dilemma.

He got a few days of leave from the base and thought his girlfriend was on her way down from extreme North Georgia to Atlanta to pick him up. That was before her job told her that she had to come in. The way he explained it, though unfortunate, sounded quite reasonable and very legit, but he wasn't buying it. "You know how those white bitches are about some good black dick, man. After they get turned out by a few, they can't keep their legs closed for just one anymore!" After quickly disclosing his name, his rank and position at Fort McPherson, he went onto further explain that his girlfriend was one of those white trash whores that he was trying to make into a housewife after he stupidly ran up in her raw and got her pregnant with a pair of twins. His paranoia led him to believe that her backing out at the last minute from picking him up meant that she wasn't finishing giving all the black neighbors their blowjobs yet.

And because he was from some obscure town eighty miles away, it wasn't like he could just hitch a ride off somebody. So his anger was based in the fact that he was virtually stuck in Atlanta with no place else to go. If I was a conniving man, I would've made him an offer he couldn't refuse, but instead made the most sensible choice to ask him where his money went since he was talking as if he couldn't get a hotel room for the night. At best, without much of a straight answer, it all went back home to his philandering girlfriend and their two children together. He tried to sooth my worry that he had enough money on him to get something to eat, but not enough to score a decent room for the night without it being a homeless shelter.

Though I had some extra money on me to put a fellow serviceman up in a room for the night, he was too full of pride and arrogance to be helped out that way. So, I did the next best thing I could do for him, which was offer to be his wingman for the day. Help him figure out some other kind of arrangement, as I rode the train with him to a variety of other spots throughout the city to help kill some time and come up with a plan. But to no avail.

When it came time for me to get ready to go home, I told him about my living situation at the motel and that he seemed sane enough to stay with me for the night … if he wanted to.

He was cool with the idea, given that he had no other real options.

So we got back to the motel about a quarter to eleven (thanks to MARTA). He rushed into the bathroom to wash the day off of his body while I climbed under the sheets in bed. We hadn't discussed our sleeping arrangements, so as a last ditch effort I called up to the front desk to ask about them sending a spare bed to the room. They wanted to charge equal to another room for the bed. I told them to forget it. I was sort of wishing I hadn't when I saw him come out of the bathroom glistening with a towel wrapped around his barely-there waist. His body was not only cut up like the Black Rambo, but there wasn't a single blemish anywhere across his golden brown skin. As I tried not to stare (or get an erection) at the network of veins popping down his huge arms and across his hefty hands, I profusely apologized for our sleeping arrangements. He just crawled right under the sheets next to me, thanked me for my hospitality, and went onto sleep.

Being that it had been such a long day for the two of us, I swore up and down that I was going to sleep straight through the night. But somewhere around three in the morning, I forgot that Montego wasn't lying next to me anymore and leaned in for a midnight kiss.

"Look, man, I ain't into that fag shit," he bemoaned groggily coming to after a few seconds of kissing back, probably thinking, too, that he was back home with his girl.

"I can respect that. Though, it wouldn't be on any fag shit if you let me take care of that for you." I said, hinting at the raging black steel pipe he was trying to hide, the one that I accidentally mistook for the other soldier that shared my bed earlier. "As a good friend told me once, 'a good mouth's a mouth, right?'"

He flinched the first couple of times I reached out for it. But quickly seemed to give in to it after I pulled the covers back and proceeded to go down on him. I knew I had Soldier Boy when I slipped the enormous head of his golden fat ramrod over my lips to the roof of my mouth where I tickled the underbelly behind his piss slit with my thrashing wet tongue. He let out such a rattle of joy that it nearly scared the shit out of me with my face buried between his legs. After the initial shock, he trembled as I slipped more of his dick down my throat, polishing it with my mouth and inhaling the clean musky-funk that brewed from his wild wiry pubes.

He then grabbed my head and fucked my face for awhile. I was cool with it at first, knowing that with his good looks and country boy charm he probably got away with that shit with some of the girls at home and on the fort with some of the female cadets. The more I thought about what I wanted to do with him earlier along with my crack getting moist at the thought of it, though, I knew exactly what I wanted to do.

"Man, I got other ideas for you to get your nutt." I offered in abandon, crawling back up next to him and pulling him over me.

When he caught my drift, rolling his hardened hand between my knee and waist, I reached for a condom and some lube in the nightstand and rolled both on his handlebar of a dick.

"Yo, you fuck it like pussy, right?" He asked with adorable sincerity.

I nodded after laughing, giving the man virgin something to go on, even if I didn't care for the comparison.

Soldier Boy didn't need any further instruction after that, locking his massive arms behind my knees and massaging his slick pipe deep into my gut. I was so open by this young soldier taking control of me like this that the natural thing for me to do was reach for his neck and bring him to me for a kiss. I was almost certain that he was going to pull away again. But I could see in his eyes, in the dark room that was barely lit by the light coming in through the parking lot, that the warm vice grip that my quivering hole had on his incredible dick finally set him free to explore my mouth. I was so turned on by his raw kisses on my lips and on my neck that I was nearly oblivious to taking him to the hilt and the short thrusts he pumped into me. I was so wrapped up in this quaint intimacy that I had to feel him nearly pull out of me and strike at my prostate again before I snapped out of this loving embrace and remembered that this was just a meaningless one-night stand.

"C'mon Army fuck," I mouthed rotating my hips back on to him. "I want that soldier fuck like you mean it!"

He quickly took his cue and worked his way from working my hole to slamming it like only a random fuck in need of getting off could.

"Oh, fuck, yeah!" I cried riding the new wave of ecstasy. "I want you to fuck me, fuck! Harder! Harder! Harder! Yeah, fuck! Dig out my guts, soldier! Oh, fuckity-fuck … s-shit!"

"You like being fucked like this, huh, punk?" He asked repeatedly in a variety of sequences, with his tight butt cheeks rhythmically clenching and unclenching beneath my dry cracked heels. "Getting your pussy taken away like a little bitch, huh?"

I hated the pussy reference, but loved the authority he used in his dirty talk just to give into it.

I clung to his thick neck, scratched his broad back, as his fat long dick worked tirelessly in my aching hole, going faster and faster, deeper and harder into me with me stroking my dick in stride. While it was true that a mature daddy would've worked harder to own my hole with more grace and finesse, the eagerness of this young buck needing desperately to get his couldn't be overlooked either, doing due diligence in putting several painstaking arches in my back, grabbing my waist, spreading my ass wider just to receive him, and slapping my outer thighs with our rocking beat banging into the wall behind us.

I didn't know that I had my eyes closed riding the feeling until I opened them and saw sweat coming down in sheet off of his face and saw his beautiful jaws clenched tightly.

"Fuck yeah! Oh, shit! Shit! Take ... my ... dick! Shit! I'm 'bout to bust this nutt!" He bellowed in strangulation, ripping his dick out of my well-used ass and snatching the condom off in kind.

His pent-up cum wad just sprayed above my slender dick with my own wad simultaneously shooting up just to meet his, looking like some bad midair collision of creamy whole milk and watery skim milk that together looked like a new kind of runny yogurt covering the greater portion of my flat stomach in the end.

Daybreak soon came, though we were both sound asleep when it did, only to be woke up by his girlfriend calling to let him know that she was on her way down to Atlanta to pick him up.

And although I rode with him out to the train station to meet up with his girl and took down the number to his private line, I tossed the piece of paper on which he wrote it into the trash can once he was clear out of sight. Although he was a soldier in the U.S. Army and knew for certain that he had a great time with me, he wasn't man enough to understand that was a once in a lifetime moment that could never be recreated. However, if our paths were to ever cross again and we're free to have another motel room, we'll definitely try to make something happen again.

GANG BANGED
By Landon Dixon

"You like it, huh?" Deet growled. "You like me fucking your ass, huh?"

Sims whimpered, getting rocked, getting cocked.

Deet had driven the guy into the ratty carpet, slamming into his ass from behind, ramming, reaming. Sims' face scuffed back and forth in rhythm to Deet's savage fucking. But his ass was up, raised way up, to take Deet's pummeling dick as deep as it would go, welcoming the heavy sawing action on his chute.

Deet clenched Sims' buttocks, tore the firm, round, white mounds apart, ripping Sims' pink manhole wide open. Into which he poured his huge, black cock, plunging it inside Sims' with a brutal intensity. Deet's face shone under the single hanging bulb, his brilliant white teeth clenched tight, huge nostrils flared and gasping for air, hips pumping, dong plowing the new meat's ass.

"You wanna join the gang, you gotta take what we dish out!" he hissed, banging his muscular dark thighs off Sims' pale buttocks, making them and the man shake.

"Yeah, fuck the bitch!" Jep yelled, pulling on his own cock.

Jep and Toot stood three feet away on either side of Sims and Deet, naked as the other two men, cocks just as hard. They were part of the initiation, watching, urging their leader on, but not daring to go for a piece of that fine, white ass – that was all Deet's to break in, for now.

Deet's pecs clutched faster and faster, as he torqued up the tempo on Sims' ass, thick, black balls slapping against Sims' hanging pink balls, big, black axe cleaving Sims' chute. They were in the converted tool shed in back of the crackhouse – the place the gang called home. There was dirty carpet on the floor, dirty pictures pasted up on the plank wood walls – of men getting fucked and fucking, lots of men, taking massive cocks in their mouths, up their asses, gulping semen, draining dicks in their shitboxes.

Jep was a tall, skinny white guy with a bony face and a shock of red hair, a long, thick, vein-popped cock. His specialty was breaking into people's houses, boosting cars and merchandise from stores. His grey eyes stared wide and unblinking, his bony right hand a blur on his length of prick, his other hand up on his chest, pulling viciously on a jutting pink nipple, watching Deet fuck Sims' ass.

Toot stood with his legs wide apart, half-squatting to get closer to the action, catch all of the smells and sounds and sights. His thick body was coal-black, his licorice cock even darker, like his puffy nipples. His mouth hung open and a neon-pink tongue lolled out, as he worked his balls with one hand, his dong with the other. "Fuck him, Deet!" he grunted, pulling hard and quick. "Fuck him!" His specialty was smash and grab work, dope dealing.

Deet thrust deep, thrust fast, his yellow, half-moon fingernails digging into the creamy skin of Sims' buttocks, body slamming against. He was bigger than the other men, bolder, smarter, top dog, always on the lookout for new recruits to use for profit and perversion. He ruled with an iron fist and an even more rigid cock.

"Oh, yes! Yes!" Sims bleated, his voice muffled by the carpet, bounced around by the pistoning prick.

"Yeah, you're gettin' it now!" Deet rasped. "You're gettin' it good!"

He impaled Sims' chute, held his cock there, hood pressing soft and hard against Sims' bowels. Then he pulled back, all the way out, leaving Sims gaping and gasping.

"No! Please! Don't stop!" Sims wailed. He twisted his head around on the carpet, pushing his ass up even higher, manhole wide and pink and glistening.

Jep and Toot stared at Deet, their hands frozen on their throbbing erections, their eyes wide with unquenched desire.

Deet laughed, plunged three fingers into Sims' ass, right down to the last knuckle. "Still wanna be in our gang?" he said, hooking his fingers inside, then dragging them up the man's chute.

"Oh, God, yes!" Sims cried, shaking violently, Deet's scraping fingernails driving him wild.

"Think the bitch's got what it takes?" Deet asked Jep, Toot, spearing his cock in between Sims' trembling legs and lifting the guy's dick with his dick. He plowed his straightened fingers back and forth in Sims' ass.

"Yeah! Fuckin' right!" Jep and Toot sounded off, grinning ear to ear. They'd be next in line for that sweet white ass, getting Sims to do any shit job they wanted done.

Deet snorted, yanked his fingers out of Sims' ass, grabbed up the man's thighs and flipped him over onto his back. Sims looked up at Deet's huge, ebony dong, his back and butt against Deet's thighs, his neck bent on the carpet, his legs hanging over his painfully hunched body.

"Yeah, he might work out," Deet said. He grinned, pressed his cock down, his bloated hood squishing into Sims' gaping asshole.

Jep and Toot cranked their cocks again, watching Deet sink his massive, glistening tool into the guy's anus. Deet went right down to the balls, plundering Sims' sphincter from above. Then he gripped Sims' quivering thighs and squatted up and down, fucking the man's ass. He went faster and faster, pile-driving the bent over, red-faced new recruit to the gang.

Sims' back cracked, his neck creaked, his eyes watering, anus getting drilled, filled and fucked. His own cock hung hard and vibrating from his loins, almost over top of his face. He desperately reached up and grabbed onto it, tugged, his other hand shooting up to cup and squeeze his hairy balls, the heated stroke of massive cock in his chute almost pounding him senseless.

Deet grunted and pumped down into Sims, sweat gleaming off his planed face and striated torso. He went fast and hard and deep as he could, his huge balls tightening with impending climax, his hammering cock surging cum-hard in the ass he was blasting. Jep and Toot matched their leader's pace, the men stroking their stiffened dicks with grim determination, fisting, twisting their nipples and balls.

"Oh, God!" Sims cried. His cock went off in his shunting hand, and white-hot semen roped out of the tip, striping his chest and splashing onto his face, coating his outstretched tongue. He opened his mouth wide as it would go with the pressure on his neck, and he shot sperm into his mouth, gulped, drinking his own river of rubbery jizz.

"Motherfucker!" Deet roared, shaking, shooting. His pumping cock was seized by Sims' clenching ass muscles, and it exploded, blasting scorching sperm inside Sims, searing the man's chute and bowels. Deet flung his bald head back and bellowed, emptying his enormous balls into Sims' anus, burst after blistering burst.

Jep and Toot crowded even closer, groaning, grunting. Jizz leapt out of their strangled dicks, showered down onto Sims' shaking body. They spouted arcing jets of semen, raining into Sims' open mouth, forcing the man to swallow even faster to keep from drowning in the salty torrent.

It was one initiation that left the whole gang satisfied.

# # # # #

Deet put Sims to work right away, peddling dope, collecting the rake-off from the male hookers that used a piece of the gang's small turf, helping Jep and Toot out with their illegal work. And Sims did a good job, doing what he was told, keeping his nose clean, and his asshole – getting reamed by Deet on a daily and nightly basis.

"You're close to becoming a full member," Deet said one night, his hand on Sims' head, strong black fingers curled into the fine brown hair, guiding Sims' sucking mouth up and down on his cock.

Deet was sitting on the worn couch in the clubhouse. Sims was down on his knees, in between Deet's legs, blowing pipe with practiced ease. "But you gotta do one more thing for us," Deet added.

Sims looked up, red lips sealed tight to Deet's night-shaded shaft, cheeks billowing with suction.

"Yeah, now you gotta bring some fresh meat into the gang – for the guys and me to use. You, too."

Sims squeezed Deet's balls, sucked cock harder and faster, hood to sack, bobbing his head eagerly.

# # # # #

"This is Manuel," Sims said, introducing the small, slim Hispanic to the gang.

They were in the clubhouse, the derelict neighborhood dark outside. Jep and Toot grinned, liking what they saw. Manuel was one sweet pretty boy, his skin smooth and caramel-colored, lips plush, face fine-featured, body almost feminine. Deet grunted, walking closer, surveying the new recruit.

"He's my … partner," Sims added, looking at Deet.

Deet stared back at him. "After two months with us, you don't got any partners. We own your ass."

Manuel blinked his long, dark lashes, looking at the four men.

Deet grabbed the young man's white T-shirt at the neck and ripped it wide open down the middle. Manuel's smooth chest gleamed, heaving under the hanging lightbulb, his nipples honey-colored, stiff in the cool air. Deet roughly cupped a pec and shot his pink tongue up against one of the buds, spun it. Manuel moaned, his lithe body trembling.

"Feedin' time," Deet growled.

Jep and Toot closed in.

Jep pulled away the tattered remnants of Manuel's T-shirt and slammed his mouth up against Manuel's lush mouth, thrashing his tongue around inside the red wetness. Toot squatted down and popped the guy's tight jeans open, tore them down. Manuel's cock hung out, low, over shaven balls.

"He's packin'," Toot breathed, staring at the smooth, tan dick and licking his lips. "For a little guy, he's packin'."

Deet grunted, chewing on Manuel's nipples, bruising the man's chest with his clutching hands. Sims stepped in behind and went down on his knees, sinking his hands into Manuel's tight, round buns. "He's built back here, too," he said, kneading the Latino's taut buttocks.

Manuel stood there and took it, getting kissed, Frenched, felt up, tongued, squeezed, grabbed, and stroked. Toot gripped the young man's dick with one hand and his balls with the other, pulling on one, tugging on the pair. Sims plied Manuel's cheeks, then pulled them apart, exposing smooth crack. He dipped his tongue in, ran it wet and dragging up from the man's balls to tailbone.

Manuel shuddered, shivered. Jep sucked his kitten-pink tongue out of his mouth and pulled on it, lips sealed tight to the slippery appendage. Deet mauled Manuel's pecs, pushed them together, slashed his tongue across both rigid nipples at once.

"Mine," Deet finally rasped, kneeing Toot out of the way down below. He elbowed Jep aside up top, pulled Manuel away from Sims' ass-licking tongue.

Then Deet kissed Manuel, mashing his mouth against the other's mouth, pressing his thick lips in hard. One of his huge hands dropped down off Manuel's chest and onto the young man's hardened cock, clutched, pulled. His other hand slid down Manuel's curved back, grasped a trembling buttock, groped.

The other three gang members watched Deet make brutal love to Manuel, stripping off their clothes and swearing as they did so. Their dicks rose up in their hands, as Deet pumped his own jeaned cock against Manuel's naked erection, thrusting his tongue down Manuel's throat.

Deet took a step back, stripped. The gang showed their true colors now, their cocks hard as life on the streets could be without a crew to support you. Deet shoved Manuel down to his knees, and the men gathered round, their dickheads sniffing at the young man's hair and face.

Deet grabbed Manuel's head, jerked it up, closer, slammed his cock into the Manuel's gaping wide mouth. He stabbed balls-deep, down the back of the throat, bloating cheeks and bulging neck with his huge dong. Manuel didn't even gag, his soft brown eyes shining up at Deet.

"Fuck!" Deet and Jep and Toot marveled. Sims smiled.

Deet grasped Manuel's head with both hands and thrust his hips back and forth, jerking Manuel's head to and fro. He deep-fucked the young man's face, plugging throat, filling mouth. Manuel hung onto Deet's pumping hips, riding the man's cock with his lips and mouth, taking everything the big dog had.

Deet pulled back in a spray of saliva. His black snake glistened, twitching. He passed Manuel off to Jep standing next to him, and Jep plunged his cock into Manuel's mouth, down the guy's throat. Jep groaned and bucked and fucked Manuel's face.

It was Toot's turn. He angrily yanked Manuel away from Jep, stuffed the Latino's face full of his cock. He yelped, bit his lip, vibrating, his dong gone, buried in Manuel's mouth and throat, packed wet and tight and pulsating for ten seconds of pure delight. Then he jerked his hips back, before he couldn't take it anymore. Toot pumped his cock back and forth between Manuel's lips, fucking face with a passion.

Sims was last, befitting his status. He had barely driven his dick deep as it would go inside Manuel's mouth, taken a few toe-curling strokes, before Deet pulled Manuel away. "Hold him up," he ordered Toot and Jep. "I'm going to fuck this boy's ass."

The pair obediently gripped Manuel's arms, as Deet hoisted Manuel's thighs. The young man was stretched out in front of Deet, in front of Deet's huge, stretched cock, up in the air, Jep and Toot gripping his arms on either side, their dicks overhanging the guy's face.

"Suck his cock!" Deet hissed at Sims. "While I fuck his ass, Jep and Toot his mouth!"

It was gang-bang fever, and everyone had it. Manuel hooked his slender legs around Deet's narrow waist, and Deet split his cheeks with cock, penetrating his anus. Deet's fingertips went white on Manuel's thighs, as he pushed his dong all the way into the Latino's sweet ass, and Manuel squeezed it tight with his sphincter. As Jep and Toot crowded Manuel's open mouth with their cockheads, jamming down and in. While Sims picked Manuel's throbbing erection up off the man's hard belly and bent his head down and sucked the prick into his mouth.

The walls of the rugged shack vibrated with the men's impassioned grunts and groans, and the stuffy air went heavy with the soiled smell of sweat and precum.

Deet pistoned his hips, sawing Manuel's chute with his cock. Manuel writhed up in the air on the end of that driving dong, turning his head first one way – to suck on Jep's shifting prick – then the other – to deep-throat Toot's pumping tool. Sims doing some deep-throating of his own, head bobbing wildly, sucking full-length and feverish on Manuel's steel-hard prick.

The frenzy mounted, Deet thundering anus, reaming chute, his entire body shaking with the frantic fucking. Jep jammed his cock down Manuel's throat for all to see outlined against the man's swollen neck, as Toot slapped Manuel's bloated cheek with his angry, spit-slathered dong. Sims gripped balls and gorged on cock. Manuel's body bounced and shuddered, cocks fucking him, man sucking him. He was the first to go off.

His mewl of ecstasy pulsed all along the length of Toot's face-embedded dick. Deet felt the clasp of Manuel's anus, all the men seeing the ripples of raw joy roll through the young man's body, Sims tasting it.

He let the first heated spurt of cum splash the back of his throat. Then he yanked Manuel's erupting prick out of his mouth, let the man fountain up into the air for his gang brothers to see. He pumped slickened shaft with his hand, Manuel blowing sperm in great, gushing blasts.

Jep and Toot watched and felt and were overwhelmed. Both their cocks crammed Manuel's mouth, spouting semen, flooding the young man's throat with jizz, spilling all over his pretty face. Deet swore and stuck deep, and shot off, splattering Manuel's sucking chute again and again and again, his big body torn apart by brutal, ball-draining orgasm.

Sims was the first to put his clothes back on. And with the others' hands still full of the gasping, quivering 'fresh meat,' he calmly drew his gun and said, "Okay, guys, drop the goods. You're all under arrest."

Deet, Toot, and Jep gaped at him, stunned. Manuel grinned with satisfaction, squirming out of the men's hands. "Throw me some handcuffs, 'partner,' and I'll cuff 'em," he said.

Sims smiled, tossed a pair of cuffs to his partner. "Thought we'd get a little action of our own," he explained to Deet, "before we put you out of action."

SWAP MEAT
By Landon Dixon

"You fuck my partner, and I'll fuck yours."

I stared at the guy, hardly believing what I'd just heard. I opened my mouth, to tell him he could go fuck himself, but he went on.

"Sebastian and I couldn't help noticing the fight you had with your partner."

The entire upscale restaurant couldn't help noticing me and Damon shouting at one another over dinner, Damon running off.

"And we thought maybe we could improve your situation."

I snorted, downed the rest of the red wine in my glass. It was cold and bitter, like revenge. "Improve? How would …"

"It would inject some life back into your relationship, your sex life," Lance stated smoothly, his blue eyes twinkling. "Mix things up a bit. Besides," he looked over at the tall redhead he'd left at the table against the wall. "Sebastian has always wanted to be fucked by a black man, and he thinks you're the most handsome he's ever seen."

I licked my lips, the liquor and compliment going to my head, the implications of the outrageous proposition flooding my dick – helped along by Lance's stockinged foot now, rubbing my crotch.

I didn't brush his foot away. He rubbed me smooth and warm, up and down my expanding cock in my dress pants. I was a handsome guy – big and broad-shouldered, with a trim waist and toned body, a tight planed face complimented by a pair of large brown eyes and full lips – and Sebastian was a carrot-topped hottie himself. He had short hair and creamy white skin, a slim, shapely body and pretty face. And the man pimping him out, Lance, was a looker himself, shorter, stronger, squarer, with grey eyes and glossy black hair, red velvet lips.

I let his proposition seep in, thinking maybe he was right, maybe such a thing would jump-start my relationship with Damon; or at least shock the little motherfucker into appreciating what he really had at home. Yeah, I was liking the idea more and more. My cock was throbbing in my pants under that stroking foot, draining the blood away from my brain, draining away my inhibitions – as I drained the glass of expensive wine Damon had left behind.

We all piled into Lance's car, Lance at the wheel, me and Sebastian in back. Damon had driven off in our car, not that I was in any condition to drive anyway, or think straight.

"Where do you live?" Lance asked, starting the car. "Where do we get this party started?"

The party already was started. Sebastian couldn't control himself. He had me unzipped and upraised and locked in his hand before his partner had even put the key in the ignition. He stroked my pulsating dong with his soft, white hand, lovingly, tenderly pumping my licorice stick from swollen balls to bloated hood.

"Umm ..." I hesitated. These guys were complete strangers. But fast becoming intimate friends – Sebastian dropping onto his knees in between my legs and drawing my cock down and enveloping the cap with his lips. "457 Wellington Place," I grunted, staring down at the sexy redhead lip-tugging on my hood.

Lance drove, Sebastian sucked, I moaned and groaned, all three of us enjoying the ride. Sebastian mouthed my knob, his cheeks billowing. Then he dropped his lush mouth lower, inhaling half my pipe in one gulp, the other half in the next heady descent.

I bucked off the backseat, my cock plunging his mouth, curving down the guy's throat. I grasped his soft, red hair for something to hold onto, amazed, astonished, electrically alive with erotic feeling. He rolled his watery eyes up at me, his cheeks bulging. And he didn't back off, keeping my cock locked down in the wet-hot cauldron of his mouth and throat.

"I told you he'd really taken a shine to you," Lance said, grinning at me in the rearview mirror.

I stared at him, back down at his partner, trembling with emotion, the awesome sexual pressure being applied to my cock. Sebastian pumped hot, humid breath out of his nostrils, all over what was left of my groin, tightening his lips and mouth and throat muscles around my pipe. It was snake-charming like I'd never experienced it before. I was ready to blow out my balls under the crushing tension.

He jerked his head up. Spit and stale air gushed out, along with my cock. It glistened dark as the night, twitching; agonizing, like me, for more of the same. Sebastian didn't leave us hanging.

He gripped my balls, propping me up huge and straight and wicked stiff. Then he flowed his lips over my hood again, down my shaft, almost right to his hand on my sack. Then bobbed his red head back up again. He was sucking on my cock, all of it, sure and sensual and deep.

I rode his head with my hands, the guy driving me wild, his partner driving us home. We arrived there all too soon.

Lance parked the car next to the curb out front, and Sebastian took one last long luscious tug on my prick with his talented mouth. Then he pressed my gleaming meat down flat against my heaving stomach and zipped me back up, the run off that zipper over my bulging, pulsing dong almost setting me off right there. But I managed to control myself, as he led me out of the car and up the flagstone path to the front door of the house.

The door was locked, the windows dark. I unlocked the door, turned on some lights, unsure if Damon was home or not. And not really caring too much. It was a big house.

I'd barely set foot inside the spacious, well-appointed living room, when Sebastian dropped to his knees in the shag and unzipped me, pulled me out and into his mouth again. My knees buckled, and my blood roared, as the man swallowed me whole, sucked back and forth with a vengeance.

Lance stood back and admired the show. I pulled off my jacket and shirt. Sebastian yanked my pants down, shot a hand up onto my chest, gripping and squeezing a smooth-shaven pec, as he gripped my equally shorn balls with his other hand, sucking and sucking on my prong.

I groaned and grabbed onto my other pec, groped it, twisted a rigid, dark nipple like Sebastian was twisting my other nipple. He sucked faster, tighter, really hoovering my meat, saliva dripping out of the corners of his wet-vaccing mouth. I quivered, cock surging with the urgent pull, balls bubbling with semen, body burning.

"God, I'm going to …"

Sebastian sucked all the way back, his lips slipping off my knob. "Please fuck me, Tyler. Please, stick your big, black cock in my ass and fuck me!"

His blue eyes pleaded, his beautiful face shining. There was no way I could deny the man. "Let's see that lily-white ass of yours," I growled.

He jumped to his feet and out of his tailored clothes. He looked even better naked. His cock was as long and hard as mine, a pale imitation in the best sense of the words. I didn't see it for long, though, because he quickly dropped down onto all-fours on the carpet, wiggled his taut bottom up at me.

Lance tossed me some lube, and I sprayed my monster erection, then Sebastian's bubble butt. He moaned, as I rubbed his silky crack with the slippery substance, briefly fingering his pink pucker. Then we both moaned, when I crouched in behind his tight-mounded ass and stuck his cheeks with my nightstick.

I hit hole with hood, pressed hard. We breathed even harder. I burst through, penetrating the resistance of the guy's ass ring and barreling into his anus beyond.

"Yes!" we groaned, my cock gliding deep into his hot pink chute.

Sebastian clutched at the carpet, his buttocks trembling uncontrollably. My thighs touched up against his buns, and I grabbed onto his hips, thrust the final half-inch, shafting his chute full-length.

"Fuck, that looks hot!" Lance marveled.

I pressed my thighs flush into Sebastian's butt cheeks, rutting my dick around in his ass. My balls slapped his bum, as I started jabbing, just giving him a taste of the reaming to come. He gasped, shoving back at me.

"Oh my God!"

I jerked my head around. Damon was standing in the entrance to the living room, in his underwear – staring at me with my cock buried in another man's ass.

"I … I … heard voices … got out of bed … and … came down …"

I opened my mouth to say something. But there was no way I could explain. Sebastian bounced his butt against me, tightening his ass muscles around my cock. There was only one way to explain – that my partner had brought this on himself. I turned back to Sebastian and pumped my hips, fucking the man's ass.

It felt great, glorious, stroking my dong in and out of that redhead's hot, willing asshole. He loved it, like I loved it, splashing his cheeks back against my hammering thighs, letting me delve all the way into his gripping chute, fucking full-length and free. And the blistering scene and sensations obviously inspired more than just me and Sebastian because suddenly I saw Lance fucking my partner out of the corner of my eye.

I fully opened my eyes. It was no illusion. Damon was bent over an arm of the leather couch, naked, his chocolate body gleaming under the lights, Lance in back of his plush booty, easing white cock into black ass. It took my breath away. I stuck Sebastian deep, stopped. To watch Lance slide his long, smooth dong all the way into my man's anus.

Lance's hands blazed pale on the dark meat of Damon's butt cheeks, as he pulled them back, so Sebastian and I could see him spearing into Damon's hole, spiking ass with everything he had. Damon lifted his head and moaned, hands tearing at the couch, legs quivering violently, like his buttocks. Lance stuffed him full, swelling that delicious bum even bigger. I knew that wonderful feeling well.

Sebastian whimpered and squeezed my cock with his ass. I pumped him again, harder and faster now.

Locking eyes with Damon, I slammed into Sebastian's butt, Lance drilling Damon's anus. My partner's amber eyes were glazed with sexual feeling, his handsome face contorted with lust. His mouth hung open pink and wet, his wide nostrils gasping for air. But we connected, communicated our love for one another, as he took it up the ass from one man, and I fucked the ass of another.

The raw, wicked situation suddenly got the better of me, and I tremored with onrushing ecstasy, ramming Sebastian. "Not yet! Don't blow it just yet, big guy!" Lance yelled from over by the couch. "We haven't explored all the possibilities for revving up your partnership – our partnership."

He eased up on Damon's asshole, gesturing at Sebastian and me to come over. We set up on the couch, Sebastian on all-fours on the cushions with his butt pushed up in the air, my cock embedded in it again, me on my knees in behind. Lance had pulled Damon erect, his own cock still buried in my lover's ass. Only now Damon's cock was hanging out, for Sebastian to suck on, as I fucked him.

And I fucked Sebastian, with renewed energy and lust, watching the guy suck on my partner's cock. I bounced him back and forth on Damon's dick, making him deep-throat my man like he'd deep-throated me, rocking him and the couch. Damon loved it, leaning back in Lance's gripping arms, getting his butt drilled from behind, getting his cock hummered up front. He shook with pure joy, ass-cocked, cock-sucked.

I gritted my teeth and sunk my fingernails into Sebastian's flesh, plugging his butt with a vicious intensity. His milky cheeks rippled non-stop, my noir cock jackhammering his chute. But he never let go of Damon's dong with his mouth, urgently sucking pipe in rhythm to my ass banging.

It quickly escalated to frenzy level, no holding back now. Lance gripped Damon's clenched pecs and pistoned cock into his chute. Damon whimpered, cried out, shaking with more than just fucking now. He was coming, jerking, jetting his hot steaming lust out into Sebastian's mouth.

It sent me over the edge. "Fuck! Fuck!" I howled, voicing it, doing it. My balls tingled and my cock exploded. I spasmed, shooting into Sebastian's sucking ass, again, and again, and again. Matching my partner ecstatic burst for ecstatic burst.

We stared at one another, jolted by joy, filling a man's mouth, filling a man's ass. It seemed to go on forever, was over way too soon. I'm not sure if Lance and Sebastian actually came or not. I only had eyes for Damon getting fucked and sucked, my other senses overwhelmed by my own wild orgasm.

Lance had another proposition, for both Damon and me this time. "Lie on the floor, Tyler," he told me. "And you, Damon, lie on top of your partner." He grinned at Sebastian. "We're going to turn up the kink another notch."

Sebastian grinned back, standing next to Lance now, his lips shining with Damon's sperm, ass leaking my jizz. I lay down on the carpet, and Damon stretched out over top of me. Our cocks squeezed together, swelled together. We kissed, Frenched, hardly noticing Lance tying up my hands tight around my lover, Sebastian tying up Damon's hands. We were locked in each other's arms, locked in love again.

Then we were rudely jarred back to our senses, when Lance suddenly said, "Good. Now we can clean this place out. Thanks, guys."

I stared up at the man and his partner.

They quickly dressed, started systematically stealing everything of value in our home. My cock shriveled against Damon's, as he glared daggers into my eyes.

"All done, men," Lance stated fifteen minutes later, he and Sebastian clutching their sacks of loot. "See, I guess I didn't explain my relationship with Sebastian all that clearly," he said, throwing an arm around the redhead's shoulders. "We're partners, all right, but strictly in a business sense. We find wealthy gay couples, swing with them, and then take away their swag and split it between us."

The man smiled at his partner in crime. "It's a pretty lucrative business, too, with some amazing fringe benefits. And the best part is, not one couple has yet to report us to the police. Too embarrassing, I guess, what with the circumstances involved, and the pictures."

Sebastian pulled a small camera out of his pocket, snapped some shots of me and Damon trussed up naked to one another. Pictures that were more than compromising to a successful businessman like me, and a two-term state senator like Damon.

I tentatively kissed my partner an apology when the pair of thieves had finally left. He softened, his cock hardened. I pumped my hips, he pumped his, and we fucked cock-to-cock in our tied-up position, nothing else to do. At least our sex life had been jump-started by the experience, our bonds of love strengthened, so to speak.

DOWN ON THE BAYOU
By Landon Dixon

The sun was blazing down, the humidity thick enough to cut with a knife. I stepped onto the dock and mopped my face with the front of my T-shirt, looking at the kid with the rod and reel sitting on the end of the dock.

It'd been a long trip down from the North, to the deep South. Heat and fatigue were taking their toll. But the plane crash information was mine exclusively for only a short time, so I had to act fast.

"How're they biting?" I called out, walking down the dock towards the kid.

The sun-bleached boards creaked under my feet, the green bayou water glittering in the sun, dazzling my tired eyes. I was wearing just the white tee and a pair of tan cotton pants, sneakers, and it felt like I was wearing a suit of armor in that sultry inferno. The kid didn't even turn his head and look at me, until I was right up in behind him. Didn't have a care or an enemy in the world, or so he wanted me to believe.

He was dressed in faded, torn blue overalls, nothing else. His bare arms and chest shone dark and smooth. His face was long, like his lanky body, his brown eyes brilliant white around the edges, nose flat at the bridge, wide at the nostrils, hair thick and black and bushy. He was maybe eighteen or nineteen. The rod and reel were brand-new.

"What's that, mister?"

"I said: how're they biting?"

He shrugged, drew back his thick, dark lips and grinned rows of bright white teeth. "Got a couple of nibbles."

I got right to the point, before I melted out there on that open dock. The trees were already swaying across the water, and not from any wind. "You heard anything about a plane going down in these parts?"

Rick Anson's single-engine Cessna had crashed twelve hours earlier, the last fix on the craft and its precious cargo within a fifty mile radius of where I was standing and sweating. The guy hadn't filed a flight plan, was deliberately not looking to be tracked. Fifty miles was a lot of steaming, thick bayou.

The kid squinted up at me. "Huh?"

I smiled, my face muscles straining with the effort. "Name's Terrance Freeman. I'm with the FAA, investigating a reported plane crash in this area. What's your name?"

He turned his head away, looking at his float bobbing in the murky green water. "Milt."

"Okay, Milt, like I ..."

"You got a badge or something?"

I slammed the bottom of my right foot into the small of his back. He went flying off the end of the dock, splatted face-first into the water. The anger just boiled out of me. I was short on time.

"Listen, punk!" I growled when Milt surfaced, splashed around to face me. "I asked you a straight question, and I want a straight answer." I towered up above him, glaring down at him.

He shook water from his shining face, his hair sparkling with it. Then he grinned again. "I don't do anything straight, mister."

He slipped the straps of his overalls off his shoulders, floated onto his back, skinned the one-piece garment right off his lean body. His cock bobbed up on the surface of the water, a black snake glistening in the sun, growing harder, getting longer.

I licked my lips, looked around. We had that enclosed section of the bayou all to ourselves, just the incessant buzzing of insects to disturb the oppressive silence. I took the bait, and plunged into the water with the kid.

My feet hit sucking bottom. The brackish water went up to my chest, nipple-level. Milt craned his neck, looking down his body, over the humped cord of cock, at me. I waded in between his floating legs and grabbed onto his prick, pulled it upright and stuffed the blue-black cap into my mouth.

He took it like a man who's taken it many times before, tilting his head back into the water and spreading his arms wide, cock seizing up harder and longer in my hand and mouth. I cupped his big shaven balls, gripping his pole at the base, and bobbed my head up and down, sucking on the water-slick pipe.

The hood was cobra-huge, the shaft wrist-thick and smooth. The kid's cock throbbed in my clasping hand and sucking mouth.

"Caught yourself a big one, huh, Milt?"

I choked on shaft halfway down, swung my head around, spinning Milt's body with me. A man stood on the end of the dock. He was short and squat, built like a black fireplug, dressed like Milt had been. He cradled a shotgun in his large hands.

"Been hunting, myself," he said, grinning. "Didn't bag nothin' – 'til now." He canted the shotgun down with his right hand, unfastened his overalls with his left. The tattered blue garment dropped down to his sturdy ankles. He picked his dick up, hefted the heavy black rod.

"My cousin – Marvis," Milt said.

Marvis nodded, gestured with the shotgun, stroking his snake.

I pulled Milt's dong out of my mouth and climbed up out of the water and onto the dock, slipped off my sodden T-shirt and pants. My own cock popped out hard and long in the steambath air.

Marvis was in his early thirties, had a square-shaped, shaven head and a hard, high-cheekboned face, narrow brown eyes and thin black lips. His compact body was ribbed with muscle, pitch-black. He meant business, had the equipment to back it up.

I dropped down onto all-fours on the dock. Milt stuck his cock in my face, Marvis stuck his cock in my ass.

I groaned, mouth full of Milt's member again. Marvis had oiled his gun, and slid it in smoothly, gliding every inch of veined, pulsing meat into my chute. The shotgun clattered down on the boards behind me, when his pubed balls bumped up against my quivering cheeks. Then he gripped my hips, pumped his, stroking long and deep and hard into my anus. Milt grasped my hair and fucked my face with his dong.

They got a rhythm going, faster and faster. Marvis pounded into my ass, reaming my chute. Milt plunged back and forth in my mouth, bending down my throat and out again.

My dizzy head was pushed up, my swollen ass pulled back. I gasped air through my flaring nostrils, burning with heat, sweating out of every pore, struggling to stay conscious with all of that meat stuffing my butt and filling my face. They gave it to me at both ends, backwoods busted style.

Milt yelped, jerked, his fingers biting into my scalp. Hot, salty semen spurted against the back of my throat, squirted out the sides of my mouth, the kid's cock jumping and spunking.

Marvis rammed my ass with a vengeance, the crack of his clenched thighs against my rippling cheeks blasting the heavy air above even Milt's cries of joy. Then he grunted, shuddered. His cock surged in my chute, shot searing sperm up against my bowels, the guy dousing me with his lust like his cousin.

I wrenched a hand off the wood and grabbed onto my own thundering wood. One stroke was all it took. I shivered in the throes of the two men's ecstasy, and my own, spilling seed all over the boards, before blacking out.

# # # # #

They showed me the plane, when it became clear I wasn't leaving the bayou until I'd found it.

The Cessna was buried nose-deep in a stagnant swamp pool about two miles north of where the guys kept a shack. They'd seen it go down, had lit out for it in their flat-bottomed boat, which now sported a brand-new outboard motor, I noticed.

I jumped out of the boat and waded through the scummy water to the plane, combed through the cabin and cockpit. I didn't find a thing – except the body of Rick Anson, still strapped into the pilot's seat.

We went back to the shack. I grabbed the shotgun when Marvis attempted to hand it to Milt, so he could go out for a leak.

"Okay, boys, enough fun and games. Where's the money?" I rasped, pointing both barrels at both men.

Milt licked his lips. Marvis grinned. The sticky, suffocating heat in the small shack weighed down on me like a living, breathing thing.

"There wasn't any ..."

"There was money! Five hundred thousand dollars that Anson robbed from the Brinks' armored car depot in Utica. Where is it?"

"Oh, yeah," Milt offered. "We turned that over to the sheriff's department, mister. When we told them about the crash."

"That's right," Marvis chimed in. "We're supposed to get a reward for recovering it."

They nodded at each other, grinning.

I raised the shotgun up to my shoulder and locked it in, tightening my finger on the trigger. "If you told the sheriff, there should be cops crawling all over this sweltering backwater, no body still hanging up in the plane. And you two shouldn't have new fishing and boating gear – until after you've received your 'reward'." I aimed the shotgun at their heads. "Go on – with the truth this time. Where'd you hide …"

"Drop it, mister!"

A third man, another cousin. His name was Malcolm. He carried a pistol, was tall and wide and coal-black, had close-cropped hair and a gold ring in his right ear. His head was huge, to go along with his body, his features thick and heavy, brown eyes hooded by sleepy lids.

"You're going to go back to where you came from and never come here again," he advised me. "No hard feelings. Unless you want 'em."

"He wants it," Marvis said, taking the shotgun from me.

I was hard, had feelings. All those men in those close, sweaty quarters, had stirred up the feelings in my loins again. And I wasn't alone. "A farewell send-off, eh?" I said, smiling good-naturedly.

They stretched me out on top of the low wooden table that occupied a third of the shack. Malcolm gripped my bare legs to his massive, muscle-cleaved chest, his nightstick pointing ominously at my ass. While Milt eagerly lapped at my nipples, ran his hands all over my bare chest and stomach. And Marvis stuffed his engorged cock into my open mouth.

I sucked on Marvis' prong, shifting my head back and forth, wet-vaccing cap and shaft. Milt spun his bright pink tongue all around my nipples, making them buzz, bud higher and harder. He sucked on them, bit into them, cupping my shimmering pecs and caressing my heaving stomach, fondling my hard cock. Malcolm pressed his lube-greased hood in between my butt cheeks and up against my pucker.

Marvis took my moan of pleasure full length along his cock in my mouth. As Malcolm squished his hood through my starfish, sunk licorice log shaft into my anus. He drilled deep as his dong was long, clutching my quivering thighs, rocking my body with cock.

Milt picked up my prick and sucked on it. I sucked on Marvis' prick, the guy guiding my head to and fro. But I hardly felt the one man's velvety mouth, the other man's oiling dong; as the biggest of the three men pounded into my ass with his sledge of a hammer, blasting my anus and body full of sensation. His shunting slammer filled me entirely, swelling my being, stroking and stoking my soul.

Milt dropped my dick and crowded in close to my head, anxious to get sucked like his cousin. The two men fed me cock in long, treacle tubes, each fucking my face in turn. As the giant gored my asshole with his ebony horn.

I knew I wouldn't walk straight for a week, be able to sit up in a chair, and I welcomed it. Excitedly sucking off two men, getting brutally fucked by a third. My eye still on the prize, all the same.

Marvis groaned and clawed at my hair. He flung his hips at my head in a frenzy, balls bouncing off my drooling chin, cock pistoning my mouth and throat. Then he howled, jetted, jizzing me. I gulped madly, voraciously.

Milt jerked my head his way, sawed my face with his cock. He cried out and creamed me, spouting his rubbery sperm right down my throat. I swallowed for all I was worth, getting showered with semen and sweat.

They twisted my head back and forth between their spurting dongs, sticking and spunking my mouth; my ass and body getting banged to and fro by Malcolm's mammoth member. The big guy cursed, hollered, ferociously splitting my anus with his axe. Then he shook out of control, muscles popping all over his gleaming noir body. Semen scorched my chute, blast after blast, squirted out of my overstuffed burning raw butt.

I came hands-free and hard as huge Malcolm. My cock leapt up off my stomach and geysered cum, Malcolm's pumping dong propelling my own lust all over my face and chest. I clung to blurred consciousness by the skin of my teeth biting into Marvis' cock.

# # # # #

They let me go with that warning never to return, that flying fucking send-off.

I returned six hours later, with a search warrant and ten fellow Treasury Agents. I'd lied to the boys about being with the FAA, but I was a member of a federal authority, with a duty I was sworn to perform.

Because if I couldn't get my sweaty hands on that $500,000 all for myself, dishonestly, pursue my dream of a life of leisure on the Mediterranean coast; at least I could recover the loot for the armored car company, honestly, maybe garner a promotion and pay raise for breaking the case.

STRIKE ZONE
By R. W. Clinger

"Nice ass, DeMarco," the third basemen for the Houston Hawks says in his deep urban intonation, surprising me. "Wouldn't mind spanking it bare if you gave me the opportunity."

I look over my right shoulder and take in Jet Locke: six-two frame, chocolate brown skin, onyx-colored eyes, sexy-tiny scar near his right eyebrow, twenty-four years old, 185 pounds of muscled jock-body. My gaze studies his adorable dimples and helplessly drops to his black-and-white baseball pants. What rocks my world is the deflated bat between his legs: two inches wide and six inches soft. Porn stuff that is longer and thicker than most guys I have ever hooked up with. A tool ready to be played with, eaten, or whatever comes first.

"Like what you see, sexy bitch?" Jet asks, chewing a wad of tobacco in the right pocket of his mouth. He takes a quick spit, moves closer to me, and adds, "Rumor has it you take dick. Is this true?"

I know Jet is just fucking with me, wanting me to make a mistake and prevent a run for my home team. Truth is, I try to ignore him and turn my stare to the fans in the bleachers: cheering on the batter Nate Moore, drinking, eating, some are even fighting. My concentration now falls on Nate at bat, one of my springtime flings from last year.

"I could press your white ass over a locker room bench and bang pickoffs out of you," Jet teases. "What do you think of that, DeMarco?"

"Try me," I whisper, toying with the brawny and black third baseman. "My ass is ready for you anytime you want it."

I think this will deter and catch him off guard. Jet doesn't flinch, though. Instead, he steps closer to me, gently reaches out and discreetly runs his right hand along my ass. "Tight and smooth ... just the way I like my base runners."

Summer sun peeks out from behind August clouds and bleeds into my eyes. It's the bottom of the ninth, and the score is tied 3-3. This game is hardcore shit. Not for sissies. Something serious. If I obtain a run, the inning will end thereafter, and we win the game. If I don't gain a run, my teammates will be pissed off at me. So I concentrate, totally into this gig, and try to become a sports hero.

Behind me, Jet tries to rattle me. "Do you like it when a guy shoots his hot load all over your back, DeMarco?"

I kind of do but decide not to share this queer detail with him. Instead, my instinct for the game kicks in. Nate hits a line drive, which prompts me to run for home plate and win the game. In doing so, Jet is right behind me, ready to tag me out when the opportunity arises.

What rises is the deflated cock between my legs as I dive for home plate. Creating a cloud of dust around me, scoring a game-winning run, I still feel Jet's straying hand on my ass, invading my privacy. Jamaican men are my weakness. Every dark-skinned man I see inevitably becomes mine for the taking. My moment of bliss is soon lost, though, when the umpire yells, "Safe!" at the top of his voice. The Dagger fans go wild, and the game ends: Daggers 4, Hawks 3.

Jet helps me up. Half of me wants him to brush the field dust off my legs, chest and cheeks with one of his hulking palms. Instead, he congratulates me on my winning slide and winks at me. Before I'm mauled by four of my excited teammates, grabbed and tousled and man-handled in a sportsmanlike way that I really don't seem to mind, he says out of the umpire's earshot, "Tonight at ten ... be in the dugout. Just you and me. I want to show you how much I like the game ... and base runners."

The hungry and besotted look on his alluring face convinces me that he isn't joking around. His coal-colored eyes tell me he wants some man-with-man contact. Black with white action. Obviously, he desires my azure-colored eyes, brown curly hair, chiseled face, and five-eleven structure. He might just be teasing me though, making me look like a fool. I'm careful not to fall into his little sex-game, or whatever it is, and say, "What if I'm busy?"

"Don't be busy, DeMarco. My cock really wants to nail your white ass tonight."

I watch him adjust the padded goods between his legs, wink at me a second time, and eventually walk away. What I'm left with is nothing less than a shiver of excitement that rocks my core, and the sight of his bulbous trunk shifting left and right in his skin-tight uniform.

The night's summer heat is stinging hot, which makes it a very sticky ambiance for a run. Decked out in a pair of Rufskin shorts and Nike running shoes, bare-chested and sweaty from a fresh sprint around the city, I end up in the Daggers' dugout at Fungo Field exactly on time. Although Jet doesn't show, I feel tonight's run is not a wash. I like to take care of my body, exercise regularly, and …

Jet surfaces out of the dark and finds me in the dugout. He sports a pair of shorts, sandals and muscle tee, which clings to his hulking torso like plastic wrap.

After studying his shadowy, well-built chest and muscled thighs, I say to him, "I thought you stood me up."

He shakes his handsomely dark head and replies, "I'm not that kind of guy."

"A guy like you should be in Houston tonight, back in his hometown. Why is our game over, and you're still here?"

He steps up to me, runs two fingertips over one of my nipples, stares into my eyes, and whispers, "Trust me, our game is just starting."

"You like what you've found, and now you're staying for overtime?"

His two fingers delicately pinch my left nipple as he replies, "Don't flatter yourself, base runner. My uncle lives in this city, and I'm visiting him for a few days."

"I thought tonight was about my white ass?"

Jet removes his hand from my nipple, closes the gap between us even more, draws our chests together, finds my tight rump with his right hand, and clarifies, "Let me feel it and then I'll decide."

I covet his palm on my bottom and his beer-scented breath on my face. Although the moment is sexy-hot and repugnant at the same time, eight inches of swollen beef comes to life in my shorts, pressing against his middle.

"Nice bat you've got going on, pal," he chants, smiling from ear to ear.

"Want to try it out?" I feel vulnerable, falling under his dugout spell.

Jet sort of chuckles. "Actually, I'll take you up on that." He draws away from me, lines my chest with some heavy kissing, swirls his tongue between my pecs, moans with bliss, and fingers the rim on my shorts.

"Go ahead and pull them down to my ankles. It's what I came here for."

In a matter of seconds I realize he's teasing me. The tasty brown third baseman is still playing a game with me, completely in control of our dugout tryst. He meets his tongue to a nipple, my navel, and now the rim of my shorts. His muddy-colored face falls to my privates, and he takes a strong whiff of my hidden and hard shaft, inhaling my sweaty stink. Jet whispers, "Bomb," pleased with my offering.

The running shorts at my waist are not pulled down to my ankles. Instead, the jock rolls his lips over my cotton-covered package in a sensually hot manner, tormenting me with his zealous antics.

Dribbles of hot cream leak out of my rock-hard shaft beneath my Rufskins. Elation is found and causes me to lightly pant. I grasp his bald head with both palms and moan, "Jet, what did you find down there?"

The Hawk mouths my goods in a hungry conduct. He works his lips over the width of my tube, runs his face in an east and west direction against the cotton, and murmurs with euphoria.

More bubbles of pre-ooze leak out of my tube and decorate the inside of my shorts. In truth, I just want to remove my palms from the back of his head, push the Rufskins down to my knees, and bang his throat with my sweet staff.

This greedy act of zeal doesn't transpire, though. Jet evidently has other intentions with my skin. Speedily he pulls away from my goods, stands again, places a tongue-driven kiss to my lips, pinches both of my nipples at the same time, and presses his swollen stick to my swollen stick.

I melt against him, over-excited and ready to burst a creamy cargo all over myself. Tamping off the urge is found, though. There is no reason to blow just yet. More sexual time is craved between our bodies before I want to shoot.

He pulls away from my face, rips off his tee, and drops it to the dimly lit dugout's bench. It gives me enough time to study his ripped chest: chocolaty-perfect with pumped dark nipples, russet-colored abs of shimmering steel, puckered navel accessorized with sprigs of sexy black fur.

"You are swollen hot," I utter, windblown by his coffee-colored beauty.

"Enough with the talk. Get on your knees and suck me off."

As I listen to his instruction, he uses both of his hands and pushes his shorts down to his ankles. What flops out of his own cotton leaves me awestruck and feeling enamored. My eyes study his six inches of limp tool, ready to be kissed, licked, and sucked. The beef is a mahogany hue, uncut and veined. I have no doubt that it measures over two inches wide and will gag me; something I look forward to.

"Take it, DeMarco," he instructs. "Choke yourself with it."

I don't have to be told twice and open my mouth with hungry ambition. Hearty sucks ensue with to and fro motion. His balls begin to thwap against my chin, and I hold their sensitive and hairy beauty in my right palm.

In less than a minute, his sword swells to a heaping nine inches inside my body, and he begins to garrote me. Painful, but fully desired smacking occurs to my face with his pelvis. His curly patch of black triangle-hair above his cock brushes against my upper lip and nostrils, letting me consume their strong and sweaty man-scent. Oxygen is soon lost by his back and forth movement as all nine inches of his protein block my lungs.

I gag and grunt and lose consciousness for a second or two. Blindness finds me, but only temporarily. My lips, tongue, and larynx go numb by his thrusts, which are mixed with my continuous sucks.

Above me, erect and in a state of bliss, Jet burbles, "Don't stop, base runner … Eat it all up."

When was the last time I was into a Jamaican like this? Why do these men of the Caribbean have such an effortless sexual power over me? What sex-spell do they concoct with my cock and mind? And, how is it possible that in their naked company, connected to their glistening-black bodies, does my shaft shoot its load without even being fondled or sucked?

Truth is, as I blow him, a gasp of excitement exits my mouth and a vibration of bliss-reaching emotion ripples throughout my core. The stiff flag between my legs explodes on its own, completely untouched and unsucked. Sticky cream shoots out of my rod and decorates the inside of my Rufskins. Juice moistens my cotton fabric, firm balls, and sweat-slicked thighs.

Jet's pelvic thrusts continue to bang my face. Pubic hairs prickle my nostrils, fall away, and prickle them again. His motion is prosaic and unstoppable above me; exactly what we both long for. In anticipation for his own sap-fest, he warns, "Almost shooting … back away."

I'm careful about sex with random buddies and listen to his instruction. He isn't at all that random, though. I've known the jock for the last two years, ogling him from game to game in our league, perhaps worshiping his tasty-dark body to the fullest, and desiring nothing less than our stinging-hot flesh to connect like now.

The all-star athlete jacks his own meat up and down with two working fists. In the gloomy light, I see veins bulge along his chest and neck. A whimper of lust escapes his handsome mouth, and his hips carry out some manic thrusting. White-splash twirls out of his erect dong and garnishes the side of my neck and chest.

Goo drips off my stiff nipples, down and over cut abs, and reaches my navel.

I do believe our tryst in the dugout is over. He will head back to his hotel room, and I will leave for home. Our flesh-meeting doesn't end this way, though. More accurately, the jetty god reaches one hulking palm against the back of my head and directs me to stand. In a matter of seconds, I'm on my feet.

Caught off guard, he leans into my neck with his open mouth, sucks his creamy treat into his system, and travels southward bound along the solid plates of my chest, finishing his job.

When he is through devouring his man-shoot, fulfilling his craving, I am patted on my rigid bottom and told by him, "Nice work, DeMarco. You're quite the team player."

Indeed I am.

"I hope your ass is just as tight as your mouth when I fuck it."

I watch him pull up his shorts and conceal his still-hard dog. As he finds his tee, I ask, "You think that is going to happen?"

"I guess you'll just have to wait and find out, won't you?"

I think about taking him back to my condo and keeping him for the night. He has other plans though, returning to his uncle's side for a nightcap. As expected, we head in different directions, but just for the time being … until we meet again.

Sixteen hours later, Jet helps himself to the passenger seat of my Porsche. I'm parked outside Around the Play, a local sports card den where I sometimes meet and greet fans. I sign cards and other memorabilia for about two hours. When the gig is over, I find my car and climb inside.

Jet shocks me by appearing out of nowhere and slips into the passenger seat. When he sits down, I take in his creamy colored-cocoa good looks and rattle off, "Hey, buddy. What's up?"

"Let's get out of here," he says in a serious tone.

I'm on it and kick the engine on.

He points to the steering wheel in a rushed action. "Take us somewhere where it's private."

We can head back to my condo, but Jet agrees it's too far away. I take him to the city's overlook on Hobb Hill where we can both consume an aerial view of Fungo Field: baseball diamond, empty bleachers, and dugouts.

Once the Porsche is parked among maples, oaks, and blue sky, I ask him again, "What's up?"

He looks to his left, right, and behind us. The place is empty. It's just the two of us in the Porsche, temporarily hidden from the judging masses. He leans over the seat and meets his thick Jamaican lips with my narrow white ones. His tongue quickly darts into my mouth. Fingers find my Lycra jersey and begin to peel it off. Before I know it, I'm out of the shirt, fully erect in my designer jeans, and ready for his play.

I let him do what he desires with my body. Why not? We've already crossed a line between league teams, right? Besides, the man can kiss: heatedly, vigorously, and with much candor. My emotions spin and twirl by his action, and allow his plump lips to travel down and along my neck where they meet a tender nipple that he gently bites.

Relaxed in the leather seat behind the wheel, I moan, "You can't get enough of me, can you?"

A grunt escapes his working mouth. He licks and laps at my nipples, works his way down and across my rigid abs, breathes in my Lever 2000 aroma against my navel, and comes up and off my stomach for air. "The thought of you kept me hard all night long. I couldn't sleep at all. I wanted to find you today and did."

"Did you follow me to Around the Play?"

He provides a gleaming smile, and winks. "You are rock-hard perfect for me. I can't keep away from you."

The getting with me is good and is accomplished in a matter of seconds. Denim buttons are popped open, and he releases my eight-inch flag, thwapping it against my ripped torso.

"Damn, you've got some nice junk here," he happily shares, reaching for my stem's base near my balls.

Two pre-bubbles of excitement leak out of my cock's cap. The pearls of ooze decorate my tight navel. The ball player is on his game and uses two fingers on his free hand to collect the sticky sap. "No need to waste the shit."

His fingertips gently slip into my semi-parted mouth. I suck on both, charged with pleasure, and consume my own gluey spurt. Jet confirms, "There are other things I would like to stick inside you."

I moan with pleasure, hungry for my own ooze, devouring his fingers as if they are two brunette cocks in my face.

"Eat it all up, DeMarco. Don't be shy."

Being timid is not an option when it comes to Jet, I realize. Effortlessly and unconditionally, I am smitten with his good looks and charm. Truth is I will do anything he wants me to do, just so I can be close to his succulent and ripped skin, greedy for our two races to mix.

I listen to him ask, "You ready for a heater?"

Hell yeah! Bring it on. I'll take a doubleheader ... curve ... brushback ... anything from him, since he's so hot for me. The jock is drop dead gorgeous, and I'd be a fool to pass up this connecting moment with him.

After being fed my own spurt, the third baseman goes to town on my rock. His left hand fires up and down on my tool while his right hand soothingly massages my balls. Like his plays on the field, being the professional athlete that he is, Jet watching the pitcher, catcher, hitter and runner all at the same time, he multitasks with my body. His mouth meets a nipple and his tongue flicks its strawberry-colored apex. More continuous north and south jerks are applied to my rod, and my balls are caressed with finger-zeal.

Frankly, I realize this encounter is not about the star-player getting off. Instead, it's all about me. I become the center of his hungry concentration and likeness. His goal is to satisfy my needs wholly while also enjoying himself. He is as attracted to me as I am of him. The only thing that prevents our bodies from becoming fully naked and connecting by rod-inside-rump is place and time. Otherwise, the promise of his inflated and veined prick would be lodged into my eager bottom, building a rhythmic climax with him.

What occurs next inside the Porsche is rather selfless of me. My greed is lost, having other intentions in mind. I push the jock's head away from my chest and his hands away from my privates. In doing so, I demand, "Get your dick out … I'm not the only one who will be coming."

An ear to ear smile surfaces on his Jamaican face. "You know the game, don't you?"

A few more bubbles of queer-leakage exits my dog and slowly drips down and along my tool – an invite for his unstoppable craving. "My rookie days are over, pal. I'm a man who knows what he wants … and you're my mark."

He takes the cue and loses his muscle tee. Mounds of brown bulkiness glimmer in the afternoon sun. Nipples the size of baseballs beam with tasty looking drops of perspiration. His chiseled abdominal also bubbles in a light sweat, constricting from his breathing. The man is a sturdy, muddy-colored god at my side; all mine for the taking at this moment.

I long for dirty, man-inside-man sex. Lips are licked as my appetite for his island skin heightens. His strike zone is what I want, and he finally knows it. It's all I can think about and want for now.

Hotness reeks from his steamy-chocolate body: the design of his packed chest, the black curly-cues of hair beneath his dented navel, and the obnoxious-size pole between his legs that affably needs to be licked or sucked. Jet is fit to the fullest degree, drug-free and top-notch perfect in every teasing way. A complete package and star player.

Helplessly I say, "You are jock-ripped to the core."

"Batter up." He has an ear-to-ear grin, pointing to his solid dong for some heavy duty action with my lips, tongue and throat, or whatever else I have to offer, satisfying his insatiable needs.

Before I go down on his extension of coconut-colored tool, I manhandle him the way he desires. My fist grabs his stiff piece of equipment and steadily moves its excess skin up and down. Numerous strokes feel like four innings on the field. My hand and his hips work against each other, deriving some hardwearing friction and gratification for the third baseman. Not that I'm complaining, of course. Having his nine inches of spike in my handy grip is not unpleasant for me. Honestly, I can't wait to see him erupt his creamy load, spraying down the Porsche's interior and my skin.

He is sent into a whirl of jubilation. His hips rise and fall in the passenger seat and he begins to murmur my name. His joint is unbending in my right hand, and its skin glides inside my palm. The baseball player continues to whisper my name, driven towards an orgasm.

I am guilty of not letting him shoot. Shame on me for being rude and thoughtless. Instead, my hand-jacking game on his beef is unstoppable. My grip becomes like a vice. Unwilling to let him fire off his load, I covet his unbending flag with my touch, toying with him.

As expected, the Hawk grunts. "I'm going to blow."

I shake my head. "Not yet … I have other things to accomplish with your dick."

A longing huff escapes his beautiful mouth. "I feel it coming, DeMarco. Sit back and let it blow."

Hell no. I have an agenda to carry out and … Jet isn't going to impede. To prove this, I remove my grip from his spike, hunch over his middle, open my mouth, and dab my tongue to the tip of his knob.

He whimpers, obviously unable to control his load. Again, he whispers my name, and adds, "Get out of the way … a wash is coming."

My action is like licking an ice cream cone on a hot day; unremitting and sloppy licks transpire before the ice cream melts. Prior to Jet helplessly shooting his wad, I take a number of licks on his timber, just as many sucks, and quickly heed his warning by pulling away before he accidentally provides me with a gluey facial.

"Unstoppable," he snivels, clamping his teeth together and providing a wide-eye stare of sexual intoxication.

"Spray it, Jet … Show me what you've got."

He finally fires out his load. Cords become hard along his neck and his pecs tighten in orgasm. Following three consecutive bolts with my fist on his erect wood, and two growls of gratification escaping his mouth, stinging hot spew fires out of his bat and decorates his chiseled and sweaty torso. Ladder-like abs and his dented navel are covered in the juice. The sap clings to his beautiful brown skin, reflecting a bright-white hue.

"That's a dinger." Jet leans his face into my mouth, takes a kiss, and groans something inaudible like an umpire calling out a foul. Happily he becomes drained, out of seed … spent.

"I like to call it a sinker." I refer to my hand job as a fast pitch that breaks downward.

Mesmerized with the moment, fully into our shared gig, he asks, "You have some fair territory?" He checks out the rock between my legs, discovers it with his left palm, fingers it with playful strokes, and begins to man-handle the protein with scorching passion.

"It's all yours." I already lift my hips off the seat and work my pick into his laborious fist. "But trust me, two more strokes, and I'm going to blow."

He laughs, ready for a last inning. His left hand is swift on my joint. Diligent and speedy motion ensues with his fist. The moving grip he has on my junk is vibrant and brisk. Fingers manipulate my skin in a rapid manner and cause me to gasp for air. Helplessly, I buck his hand a few times, and murmur the score between us. Now, I whisper in a rugged manner, "Blowing soon."

"Let it fly," he coaches, continuing his fierce but pleasurable stroking.

I respond with a grunt and groan, fire my hips upward, and heavily breathe, windblown for just a second ... two seconds ... three seconds, and feel as if I will pass out. Sweat lathers my forehead, cock and his hand. The perspiration is thick and shimmering. Another vibration of pure delight skirts through my entire torso. "I'm ready for a tater, Jet. Bring it on."

"A homerun it is," he chants, sending me into orgasm with his busy hand-work.

Frankly, I've never felt this way about a guy before: lust-driven, sexually connected with a sense of rightness, and uninhabited with his skin, desiring more and more of his naked bond. Easily the third baseman can become my boyfriend if he wants to, but only time will tell for sure and ...

"One last brushback for you, DeMarco," he whispers, stroking my meat a final time.

My load is titanic in volume. A gallon of ooze erupts out of my plump cock like fireworks after winning the World Series.

Sap ejects from my staff, spirals in mid-air, and splats against my chest. Rigid nipples and abs are decorated with the glue. Strong thighs and hips become varnished with the shit. And before I know it, like Jet, I am weakly spent and fully drained by our connection.

As Jet feeds me my own gunk–a bittersweet treat – he informs me, "I'm not leaving town until you give me a backdoor slider, DeMarco."

"I think I can arrange that." How willing I am to nail his bottom just the way he wants me to.

"And if it's good enough … I might move here and play for your team."

I let out a tangible laugh and supply, "You already play for my team."

He torments me by yanking my dog again. When more bubbles of post-ooze drip out of the tool's cap and onto his hand, he clarifies, "Team DeMarco and Jet … I like the sound of that."

OFFICER, I DIDN'T MEAN TO
By R. W. Clinger

I see the blue/red/white lights behind me in the rearview mirror, autumn all around, patrol lights that mix with red/yellow/orange. I prattle, "Right on, man. I'm right here waiting. Bring it." I want a ticket, pick up some more speed, and push the pedal to the metal. I have just blown through three red lights in the city, and head for the fourth one.

Let my game begin.

A city cop follows me, is right on my ass. The city pigs are the best of the worst for my selfish needs: bulky, meaty, burly, and always over six feet tall. Hardcore tough with aggressive hunger in their eyes. Naughty dudes with military backgrounds. Their reputations suggest a sense of pure roughness and cruelty, bitchy bad boys with bounding muscles. They are usually big, and have fear in their voices, or posted across their broad, hairy, and dark chests. You fuck with them, and they will surely fuck with you back.

I pull the bright red Mustang over to the right side of the road, flick on my four-ways, and watch in my rearview mirror with ease ... perhaps even with a sense of contentment.

The blue-purple sun blocks the view of the pig behind me. I rub at my rock-hard cock in my shorts and try to push it away. My view of the flashing lights behind my Mustang is a total turn-on. I lift Oakley shades from my face and place them on the passenger seat. Autumny air from the evening rolls in the Mustang's open windows. I take a minute to prep my hair and face, look into the rearview mirror at myself: vivid blue-violet eyes, dark chocolate-colored skin, rough boy looks with an edge that is very wild and unrefined, gold hoop earrings, thick cords in my pumped neck from working out, eighteen years old. Yes, I'm everything a cop wants. I'm badass Arnell "Ace" Jackson with attitude and good looks, chiseled and perfect. A street god with an appetite for men, particularly city cops.

Rule #1: Never let him know you're afraid of him. He can smell your fear like a dog. One ounce of fear will alter the game and ... he won't fuck you.

Cop is bigger than big: six-three, wide as a truck on top, massive structured shoulders like some skyscraper. He has a very thin waist, thick thighs all packed into his gray trousers. Mr. Cop leans over and peers into my window at me through his silver, reflective lenses. His chest looks as if it is going to pop out of his gray uniform, breaking buttons and badge and packed heat. His clean Marine hair-cut is slicked back with gel, short and streaking black, accessorized with very thin eyebrows. Cop removes his shades, and I take in his almost-black eyes that glow with an impromptu act of desire. The man from the Congo is slender, dark muscular steel, has a long nose, and is totally delicious looking. His chin is round and his eyes are somewhat oval, sexy as hell. He's about twenty-eight years old, well experienced regarding roughing up a number of guys, needy of a Nigerian man like me to enjoy and mount and throttle and gag on his pole.

He taps his silver pin against his clipboard in an intimidating manner. His other hand is busy while he gently cups his gray-covered balls and stares down at my dark chocolate deliciousness in the Mustang. Cop focuses on my bare chest, Nike basketball shorts, eyes up the package of interest between my legs, smiles, and sports his own cock-of-the-block attitude.

I look at his name badge. It glints silver and reads: T. Pound. I try to smile but can't, I don't want to like him too much; sex is what I want/desire/need, a fuck session between dudes on a back street in the city.

Pound breathes me in and takes in my perspiration from basketball practice. If he leans forward, I will let him press his crotch into my face, so I can consume and relish a smell of his man-goods.

His words are gruff and to the point. "You know how many laws you just broke?" He keeps his eyes on my bare chest and studies my firm nipples. Again, Pound eventually drops his view to my legs and seems very much interested in the crotch-inflated area between my thighs.

I shake my head and begin, "Officer, I didn't mean to."

My eyes catch on his meat-filled crotch outside my window again. The mound causes me to lick my plump red-lined lips. I see his pistol beside outlined cock. I see handcuffs and his Billy club ... or Ace club. I can lick his gray slacks and hidden man-pusher if I want to; this is how close Cop is. I can gently touch my tongue to his loaded, dark gun if he permits me to. I can ...

Rule #2: Set your expectations high. Make your own rules. Remember, you're ass is on the line. Not his. Fuck him if he wants to call the shots.

"You could have killed someone driving like that." He isn't angry at me, merely willed to set me straight, put me in my place, and make sure that I am a law-abiding citizen who is safe on the roads in my Mustang.

"I was in a hurry ... I don't know what I was thinking." The urge to reach out and touch his covered meat is conveniently overwhelming. I hold my composure together and decide to stay in the Mustang.

I'm asked to present the meathead with my license and registration, which are both up to date and legal.

Pound reviews my documents, takes some notes on his clipboard, and passes me back my identification cards. He gawks mysteriously at my hard cock in my basketball shorts, licks his lips once, twice, and now pulls his glance away from me. Something questionable lurks in his behavior that makes my firm cock twitch in my shorts. He asks in a serious tone, "Do you know how much this fine is going to be?"

I'm too turned on by him to answer. I have the ability to see the future, and I know he's going to sock it to me ... whether with his tongue, the Ace club, or his meat-probe, Cop is inevitably going to carry out some guy-nasty with me. I don't stand a chance in hell with the stud, or getting out of a ticket. The dude will probably slam me and rake me over hot, dark coals with his steamy-solid body pressed against mine. His tone is too obnoxious and significant, too godly and filthy and terrifying; an octave that only causes me to be more horny.

But I have to try and talk myself out of this mess or he will surely take my license away from me for the next year. Pound can ruin me if he wants: toss my wrists into cuffs and tote me to jail; beat the fuck out of me and leave me for dead. In the meantime, he keeps his eyes on my hard, ten-inch slab of meat covered in shorts. He takes in my sweaty forehead, boy-toy face, and chiseled chest. I use my goods and my suave manner, and somewhat boyish eighteen-year-old manner to obtain freedom, and say, "Really, Officer, I didn't mean to. Can we talk about this? I'm sure there's a way of getting me off."

Shit! I say getting instead of letting, and now ... now he's going to really plaster me with a ticket. Now Cop is going to ...

He rubs his bulging and throttling cock, reaches into the car and touches my lips with his massive fingers. Pound tells me to take a sniff of his fingers, and adds, "Is there a way I can forget about this incident?"

"Piss off." It's the right thing to say to the hottie cop to get my ass kicked ... or even licked. Words that are purposely said. My form of instigation to finally get under his skin.

Rule #3: Tease him. Don't ever give in too quickly. Play with him until you can't play anymore. Make him work for you. If he's gay, he'll play.

He tells me to get the fuck out of the Mustang.

I don't listen to him. Why the fuck should I?

Pound yanks my door open, lands a palm on the back of my neck, and yells, "Get the fuck out the car!"

I don't move. Why the fuck should I? Especially since I want to be man-handled by him. There isn't anything wrong with proving to him that I'm a young man who just happens to like being tossed around.

He rips me out of the Mustang and roughly throws me against the hood of his cruiser. Pound wants to bang my head off the metal hood and give my ass a hard spanking, but he knows I'll press charges against him. Instead, he rubs his goods against my bottom, takes a long whiff of my neck, and chants into my right ear, "You're a tease, Ace."

I'm not really sure if I feel his cock, revolver, or Billy club against my rump, but I know I enjoy it – whatever it is. Pleasure finds me as I back into his middle, rub my ass against his tool of choice, and begin to moan in a state of pleasure.

He cuffs me now, pats me down, and informs, "Don't mess with me. I gotta see what I'm in for." He rolls fingers up and down my sides, reaches around me, presses the fingers into the bulging area of my crotch, and carefully devotes his skills to my succulent body. "Not bad ... Not bad at all. Your bark is much worse than your bite." Pound now tosses my bad-ass self into the front seat of his patrol car with the cuffs still on my wrists.

"Where are you taking me?"

"None of your business."

"Are you arresting me?"

"Something tells me that you'd like that."

I become quiet and watch him taxi me to the parking lot behind the abandoned library across town. He sports an erection that won't let up in his pressed uniform. He leaves the handcuffs on me, parks, and now retrieves me from the patrol car. Pound faces me and prompts me to stand up against the closed, passenger door with metal to my back. "You wouldn't run away from me, right?" He manhandles one of my solid pecs with some mighty force, rolls a massive fingertip down to one nipple, across my cinnamon-colored abs, and pushes his hand into my shorts where he starts to play with my street goods. The guy gives my junk a firm yank. His look tells me that he wants to slap my face to see if I'm paying attention, but he doesn't carry this fantasy out. Instead, he briskly adds, "I know your game. You were speeding and went through those stop signs on purpose. A guy like you craves cop-cock and can't get enough of the shit."

I mumble with force and lust, "No ... Really, I didn't mean to do that back there. Can't you ..."

He places two fingers on my lips, shoves one into my mouth and the second one follows. His other hand toys with my right nipple and provides it with a hefty twist, release, and twist again. When Pound finally drops his fingers from the pointed flesh, he lowers his head to the nipple and begins to bite at it, pulls it with his white teeth, sucks on it, and moans with man-delight.

Of course, I'm still in the cuffs, barely able to move. I gently roll my head back and cause the tiny sticks of hair on his pointed chin to caress the jock-delicious skin on my ripped chest. Pound rolls his hand to my crotch, pushes my balls together with a cupped hand, and prompts me to groan out of pleasure mixed with light pain. In doing so, he whispers, "This is part of your fine. You shouldn't have been driving that sloppily and know it."

He doesn't give me time to answer, though. Instead, Pound dives back onto my nipple and yanks at it with his sharp teeth. He rolls fingers over my shorts-covered package and deliberately turns me on, causing me to smoothly smile and begin to pay my dues for breaking laws.

Rule #4: Act accordingly. The game always changes. Make snap decisions to benefit your ass, of course. Always be on guard. Determine when to respond to your needs, and his, in a sexual fervor.

"If you don't run off, I'll let you out of the cuffs."

Half of me wants to stay in the cuffs, so I can be his meat-puppet. The other half is bubbly and hard and wishes for my hands to stroke him off, press fingers into his Congo-colored skin, rip the uniform off his sleek and well-designed body. "Free me, Pound. I'm not going anywhere," I answer bluntly.

He listens, but he's apprehensive at first, pulls me away from the patrol car, presses me against his hard chest, slams his mouth to my semi-parted mouth, dives his tongue into my throat, comes off for air, and promises, "Next time it will be my cock shoved into you." His raging and beautiful dark eyes tell me that he wants to knock some sense into me: a slap to my face; his cock jams into my throat; my nipple pressed between his biting teeth. These actions don't transpire, though. Instead, he gives my ass a little man-squeeze before he sets me free from the cuffs, and says, "Unbutton my shirt for me."

Handcuffs drop to the asphalt of the parking lot; I rub my wrists with minor pain. Next, it becomes only natural for me to slip fingers over his steel-colored buttons and black tie, which I promptly undo. Both his shirt and tie drop to the asphalt. I now remove his T-shirt as he requests, peel it off his robust skin, and add it to the pile on the asphalt. Facing him, I study his cocoa brown-colored chest in the twilight's dim glow: lined abs, pert nipples, strings of onyx-black hair under his dented navel. Helplessly, I lean forward, discover one of his firm nipples with two fingertips, and supply it with a pinch.

Pound bucks his clothed thighs and cock into me, and touches his hips to mine. My fingers find his black belt with all its accessories, and I drop it to the ground. He lets me unbutton the top button on his slacks and …

He finds my face with his hulking palms, pulls my mouth to his mouth, and allows our heated tongues to arrest each other in a contemptible condition of intoxicated, man-with-man bliss.

After the spine-clenching kiss, Cop pulls away, and informs, "Laws aren't made to be broken."

Rule #5: Laws are always made to be broken. Lie, cheat and steal … just to get to his skin. Remember, a city cop is one of the hottest guys your ass wants. Do the crime, pay the fine. If you're not man enough to pay your dues, don't fuck around with the law.

I run hands along his bulky arms, through his onyx-black hair, and over his sweaty-slick chest. His nipples glow with utter perfection as I pull the curly strands of hair beneath his puckered navel. I touch his lower abs, a hip, and say for effect, "I shouldn't be doing this ... I should be getting home. My roommate is going to wonder where I am."

"You have a fine to pay first. People break laws and there's sacrifices involved. You're not going anywhere until you're finished with me here, man."

I play hard-ball and bad-ass all the way. I lean into him and roll my tongue along every inch of his chest in a teasing manner. Once my gig is accomplished, I rattle off, "You don't plan on using the Billy club on my asshole, do you?"

"It almost sounds like you're begging for it, Ace." He rolls his fingers over my lips, down into my shorts again, and finds exactly what he is in search of. He now frees his hand and unties my shorts, unleashes the head of my slicked cock, a long dark shaft that is already eight inches hard, and now my dangling free-for-all balls.

"Keep your fucking queer hands off me, pig."

He chuckles. I'm his gay game and he knows it; absolutely nothing can keep the two of us from meshing, I realize. I become the man's city find, and his jock to fuck tonight in the abandoned parking lot.

One of his hands squeezes my balls and cock. Pre-leak spurts out of my dick's head, and Pound's eyes seem to light up. Something tells me he wants to bend over and lap up the ooze. Instead, he simply smiles and says, "You need to show me some respect. Do you understand that?"

My answer is simple, to the point, and quite gruff. I honestly don't even realize what comes over me. "I need to show you my ass, motherfucker. Now, are you going to give me a ticket or not?"

"You bet your hole I am," he responds with a greedy smile, which tells me he isn't lying, ready to fuck my brains out.

Rule #6: If you have to beg, then beg. On your knees. Over the hood of his cruiser. Beg until you get what you want.

"You have the right to remain silent, queer. Anything you say or do will be held against you in my court of law."

"Fuck you," I breathe, and now roll my fingers through his crew cut again, over his warm head, and down his spine and splayed muscles. I challenge my fingers to touch every pore along his back as he cups my balls with a firm grip, locks his fingers onto the pair, pulls them down with fiery need, and begins to swirl his cupped palm around their furry orbs.

"Criminal," he chants rather rudely, forcefully, and drives me mad with erotic simplicity. "You need to be fucked. You know that, right?"

I need to feel all ten inches of his hard and hot flesh inside my man-canal. I need my fine paid in full, and my asshole reamed out. Mercilessly, I mention, "I could have your badge for this."

It's the wrong thing to say in the right place and at the right time. Cop turns infuriated with me. His breathing pattern becomes like a bull's: huffing and puffing and wild. I immediately feel his slick eyes against mine. The hidden cock behind his uniform becomes hard against my right leg, and his long tongue and narrow lips close over mine. Following his kiss, he pulls away quickly and his words sting me, like the essence of his cock: "I'm going to make you apologize for that. A guy like you has to learn a lesson about life. I'm the man to fuck that lesson into you."

"You don't have the balls," I respond with a lie, because he really does have the biggest balls I've ever touched.

"You honestly want me to hurt you, don't you?" He sinks his teeth into my nipple, my neck, and one of my lips. I taste his fire, attraction, and high energy, everything that makes him butch and muscular, everything that fills him with steamy hot testosterone. "Lessons are to be learned tonight. Speeding lessons. Fuck lessons."

Rule #7: Play his rough game. Don't be a pussy. He wants to piss you off; this is how he plays. Keep strong. He'll be turned-on by it. No, both of you will be turned on by it.

He spins me around and tells me to press my hands against the hood's smooth surface. I become Pound's bait, his need, his evening meat-hole. He has me over his cruiser, and I can't go anywhere, but I'm perfectly content with this action. He wants to find things hidden in my fuck-hole; maybe a weapon or something like that, drugs or money. I have nothing hidden on me though, except for my deep desire for the man to fuck me.

After he plugs me with two of his fingers, minus the lube, and finds nothing, he accidentally causes a few bubbles of pre-leak to dribble out of my hose and decorate my navel.

"You're going to hurt me, aren't you?" I inquire, trembling with sexual fire.

"Only in your ass."

Pound now rolls me over onto my back and balances me so my body won't fall off the cruiser's hood and land on the asphalt below. He eyes me in a clever manner in the faded darkness, smiles with heated desire and cop-lust, and whispers, "You should have never thought of speeding."

He doesn't give me time to answer. Instead, he spreads my legs wide and wider. Both of his large palms discover my pecs and supply them with twists. Afterward, he pulls me toward him and demands, "Hold still."

"You can't do this to me ... I have rights," I beg, impractically.

"I'm doing my job, man. Don't start with me. You keep your position, and I'll do my job."

I have the right to remain silent.

I have the right to bear arms.

I have the right to ...

I show off my clean ass for his eyes only, and for his cock's use. Sweat forms all over my body as his sleek shadow hangs over-top me. I become his prey that is in high demand, needed pleasure for the man, and for me.

He finally drops his pants, ready to force me to pay my fine. Cop snatches onto one ankle, holds it tight in his large hand. Pound man-handles his ten-inch dick with his other hand and moves his hips closer to the car, touches his droopy man-sack at the edge of the front hood and flesh meets summertime-warm metal. A growl escapes his mouth and he adds, "Look at me while you pay your fine." He pinches his cockhead to the opening of my tight ass, pushes it into me ... six inches, seven, eight ... all of its ten inches inside me. Now, he begins to pump it to and fro, fast and faster; at least he uses lube and a condom (he's done this before). Cop-cock bangs my insides with greed and an unstoppable hunger.

"Jesus," I whimper in pain, tense and hard on the hood, legs spread wide with him inside me. Above us is twilight: purple-blue-red clouds and a new moon. I want to howl like a werewolf, but need to keep semi-quiet, so we are not caught here in the abandoned parking lot.

"Hang on for the ride, pal," he coaches, continues to push and pull his shaft inside me, which causes guy-suction between us, and leaves me feeling stoned and considerably numb.

"Jesus," I whimper in pain again; it feels like his Billy club is inside my ass instead of his cock.

"Jesus doesn't have anything to do with this. This is all about the law. This is your ticket for speeding and going through those red lights." Pound semi-withdraws his meat from my lust-canal, but doesn't take it out the entire way. He shoves it quickly back into me, even harder this time, continuously, and rams me with every inch he has to offer with a desirable grin spread over his handsome face.

Rule #8: This is a man's game. Take his cock like a man. Every guy who plays the field knows this. Man it up and ... get nailed. You're not a boy. You're a man. Don't forget this.

I can't move beneath him, feel crippled and lost. "Payment enclosed," I whisper out of mere wit, desire, and need.

"Not just yet," he mumbles in return. His chest is slick with a built-up sweat, and his armpits smell meaty and masculine. He rocks inside me, bucks wildly, and calls me names like: Race-boy, Metal-teaser, Cop-pleaser. Pound pumps me hard, with much power. Blast after rough blast ensues. And, he grunts above me with utter simplicity and satisfaction. "Take every inch of me, Ace. Ride it out."

I grunt with pleasure, hidden in the night, very much aware that our cock-to-ass connection is totally unseen and unheard. I cry as he continues to pump and slam my behind.

He rushes into me again and again. His hips touch the back of my thighs, and his balls smack off my tight ass. "This is what you want," he says as he shifts his right hand up and down on my cock, prompting speedy vibrations to ripple through my perspiration-covered body.

My hips buck up and down with his movement. My ass is consumed with his throbbing meat-cork as he pumps into me with chaotic motion. The cop's tangles of pelvic cock-hair brush against my balls, swing away, and brush against them again. The badass arches his back, grins madly down at me, wild-eyed and on fire, obviously in a state of man-euphoria. Within seconds, he begins to jerk me off with his right palm, and works the excess flesh on my stick in a speedy up and down motion.

"Fuck!" exits my mouth and floods the parking lot.

"You going to speed again?" he asks, and slams into me.

"Yes, sir," I reply, grit my teeth, take everything he has to offer, and push my dick upward, into his moving hand.

Rule #9: Be careless and unruly. If you have to bark like a fucking dog, do it. You're his toy. Be a toy. This is what the game is all about. These are the rules. Don't fuck them up.

I come first; my game is almost over. I whisper something I can't remember, something unintelligible to him, something wild and untamed, and become dizzy under his hex, lost and bemused.

He thrusts hips forward, into me, pulls out, and thrusts inside me again. These actions occur more times than I can possibly count or imagine. Gooey white cum flies out of the slit of my cockhead, sputters all over his thick chest, tight navel, his black nipples and neck. The whiteness of my cum glints and hangs miraculously in the new twilight as it drips off Pound's torso in filthy strands. The ooze is thick and sticky and accents his black and chiseled flesh.

Eventually, he releases his fingers from my stiff flag and keeps up his end of the bargain. The officer of the law wants to soak my ass (inside and out) wet with his man-juice, but this idea is unsafe. Instead, he bucks into me another ten times, pulls my legs apart for a swifter ass-entrance and exit, begins to writhe above me, and inside me. Last pumps are carried out to my bottom; I can feel his cock spray white seed into the condom that separates our systems, flooding the plastic, which prompts the man to become spent, drained, empty of his load.

Rule #10: Be safe during the game. Life is too short. Always play hard, but play real and safe. Don't ever let him shower your ass with his cream. Barebacking is never part of the game.

He's not done with me yet; I know this. Face to face, the cop asks, "You meant to speed and go through those red lights, didn't you, Ace?"

I nod my head, smell the two of us mix as one, and adore the moment with him. Lost here, I feel mesmerized by our two bodies sealed together in the dark hour. Now, I find the courage to whisper, "Officer, I really did mean to."

Pound replies by kissing my forehead. He pulls away from me, sweetly cups my chin in one of his massive palms, breathes in my post-sex sting, and adds, "I want to play your filthy game tomorrow, too. Plan to break a few more laws. Don't let me down, Ace."

I agree. Why wouldn't I? Pound is why I play the game, my desire, hot-black fire. My ass craves him tonight, tomorrow night, and the night after. He is the game, ultimately.

Rule #11: Make him drive you back to your Mustang or apartment. Invite him to spend the night with you for a second fuck-fest, and wake up the next morning in his arms with your lips and chests touching, before you share breakfast, together.

LAWYER'S DARK HOLE
By Jay Starre

Kevin was supposed to be focusing on the divorce papers his lawyer just slid across the broad oak table toward him. Even though it was a very serious matter and he should have been elated that his messy divorce was soon to be over, he could only think of his stiff dick throbbing in his pants – and the gorgeous brown eyes staring into his from across that same table.

"Best deal you'll get under the circumstances. Marsha's team were pretty unscrupulous."

He understood what Stanley meant. He'd been caught red-handed by his wife's private investigators with one cock in his mouth and another up his ass. The cocks he'd been riding both belonged to those same private investigators. As a sports star, this was not the kind of thing he wanted going public. His wife had him by the balls.

Of course his lawyer, Stanley Perkins, was aware of this unsavory fact. He'd dealt admirably with the veiled threats of blackmail from Marsha's lawyers. The guy had saved his career, and as a bonus it looked as if he wasn't getting screwed out of the bulk of his future paychecks.

He signed the papers with a determined flourish and then slid them back across the table. "It'll cost me less to pay her off and give her a monthly check than it does now to live with her. Awesome."

Stanley grinned, pearly-white teeth flashing. "I admire your ability to look on the bright side."

The red-head grinned back. "And I admire your ability to contend with those other asshole lawyers and my very bitter ex-wife. Is there any way I can show my gratitude? Other than that fat paycheck your firm's getting?"

"How about season's tickets – and box seats? I love watching you out on the ice. You skate like a devil with wings."

They both laughed, eyes locked. "Consider it done. But I was thinking along more personal lines."

The innuendo hung in the air while Kevin's heart beat a little faster. He had no idea if his lawyer was bi, or gay, or maybe even just receptive to a blow job from a hockey star. But his hopes were up considering how Stanley had never commented negatively on the fact Kevin apparently liked cock so much he'd risk his marriage over it. They had viewed the private investigator's seedy camera phone video together. Twice.

The lawyer was not only good-looking, but also he was tall and slim and always immaculately dressed with grey or olive suits that set off his dark skin. Big brown eyes and a broad, full-lipped mouth dominated his square-jawed countenance.

Being a hockey player, virtually all of Kevin's teammates were white. And he'd actually never had sex with a black dude. Stanley's dark skin was a total turn-on.

"The door is locked. No window washers are scheduled for today, so we have complete privacy," Stanley replied with a smile.

The wall of windows behind his lawyer faced the Hudson River thirty stories below. Only a window washer would have been able to spy on them, or the passing plane. They did have complete privacy.

If that meant what he thought it did, it was time to make a move. It was mid-afternoon and daylight flooded the room. This was no darkened seedy hotel room, or furtive back alley at night, or deserted change room behind a wall of lockers that hid him from discovery. This was broad daylight. Could he do it?

Stanley's dark brows rose as he cocked his head and smiled even more broadly. Was he making a joke? Not likely.

Used to making split-second decisions on the ice, he went for it. Lightning quick, too, he launched himself over the table to land half on the table top and half on the startled but laughing lawyer.

Nearly as quick, the lawyer grabbed Kevin's shoulders and held on just in time to prevent his chair from tumbling backwards. "In the mood for a celebration?" he asked, dark eyes staring into pale ones.

"Fuck yeah. How about a shot at sucking your dick?"

"Go for it. I have to warn you though. It's a mouthful."

Perched on his knees on the edge of the table top, the hockey star buried his head and shoulders in Stanley's lap. He reciprocated by lunging upward with his hips to shove his crotch in Kevin's face.

Both men scrambled to tear open the lawyer's fly, unbuckling, unzipping and then yanking downward on the well-pressed grey slacks, then the purple silk boxers beneath.

"Oh my God! It's a fucking whopper!"

"I told you. Most guys can't get much of it their mouths. Or up their asses."

The big bone rearing up from Stanley's lap was about a foot long and as thick as one of those fat salamis you see hanging in the deli. The head was a flared cap that looked as if it could tear a dude in two!

He noted Stanley's mention that most "guys" couldn't take his big dick and was encouraged that the hot lawyer had at least tried it with other men. Well, he certainly planned on doing his best to show him how good a dude's hot mouth would feel around his big tool.

He came off the table at the same time Stanley pushed back on his chair, the wheels propelling them towards the windows behind them. Landing on his feet in a crouch, he wasted no more time in conversation.

He dove for that black boner. It jerked upward in an eager dance that testified to the lawyer's own lust. Kevin kissed the dark head, his pink lips soft and fluttering at first as he explored the girth of that knob, then opening wide to suck in as much of it as he could.

His first taste was gut-churning delicious. Kevin's soft lips and wet mouth had instantly released a spurt of precum that Kevin eagerly lapped up with his tongue. He dug into the broad piss slit to urge it out and was rewarded with more of the tasty juice.

He wrapped both hands around the base, excited by the pulsing feel of all that thick black meat. He continued to suck on the giant head as Stanley jerked and heaved on the chair under him.

"So good! So damn good! Your pretty pink face looks so hot buried in my black lap. Love it!"

Kevin gurgled his reply, not surprised by what the lawyer had said. He'd been told often enough that he had a "pretty" face for a dude. With carrot-red hair and brows, a pink complexion, and a small reddish goatee that surrounded bowed pink lips, he was deceptively delicate-looking. That look served him well on the ice. He darted in and out of the opposition with ease, smiling sweetly as he slammed the puck into the net past a startled goalie.

And just because he was sucking dick didn't make him a passive bottom. The deeper he sucked in that giant black bone, the more he wanted. Releasing his grasp on the huge shaft, he reached down to seize the lawyer's slacks and shorts and yank them down and off. His dress shoes slipped off along with them, and in an instant he was naked from the waist down, other than his brown dress socks.

As he gobbled up that huge dick head and a few inches of the dark shaft, he grabbed the backs of Stanley's thighs and pushed them up and back. Even though he was loving that dick in his mouth, he was thinking of the black balls and black ass below.

"Want a crack at my butt? You can eat it out before you fuck it. Go ahead, taste some dark hole."

The crouching hockey star shuddered all over. Eat that black hole? And fuck it? He couldn't believe his luck. He sucked noisily on the big shank in his mouth while his hands explored the spread expanse of that dusky butt, and he contemplated his mouth doing that next.

The silky-smooth flesh was totally hairless except for a curly thatch just above the rearing cock. Warm and solid, the thighs were substantial but lean compared to the plumper globes of that splayed ass. Even in that position, spread wide, the fullness of the mounds was apparent.

And in the middle, he found the dark hole. Puckered anal lips instantly responded to his strumming fingertips by pouting outwards. The feel of those eager lips against his fingers excited him so much he dove so deep over the cock in his mouth he nearly gagged. The flared crown plugged the entrance to his throat as he snorted for air.

"Try out my hole for a while, then maybe you can deep-throat my cock to the balls."

Kevin thought that was an excellent idea. He allowed the fat tube to slip out of his mouth with a smack of his pink lips. Glancing up into Stanley's eyes, he was pleased at how intent they looked, dark and focused under those straight black brows.

The afternoon light flooded the room, and he stared at that big butt spread out in front of him in all its glory. The cheeks gleamed like obsidian while the hole had a slightly purplish flush.

"Fuck! I gotta taste that hole!"

"It's all yours, Kevin. Let's see what you can do with that tongue of yours."

He dove into it, spreading the lips apart with his fingers and immediately probing with his tongue. The musky taste had him flushing all over and breathless. It was his first black dude and his first black hole, and he was totally keen on getting the most out of it. He sucked with his lips and tickled with his tongue as he pulled the dark lips apart with his fingers.

The hole pushed outward and gaped open for him. He drove his tongue as far into it as possible, slobbering and moaning. Firm hands grasped the back of his neck and held his face tight against that seemingly bottomless pit.

He tongued in and out, deeper with every probe. He just couldn't seem to get enough of the wet pit, stabbing at it while stretching it apart and then sucking loudly, followed by more probes with his tongue. The steamy taste on his lips was driving him nuts.

He lurched up out of that hole, the hands on his neck allowing him a brief respite. They remained firm though as his lips glided upward to suck in the dangling nads just above that wet hole and below the gigantic shaft. He sucked in one smooth ball and lapped around the giant nut, then sucked in the other so that his mouth was stuffed with both. He spit them out and moved upward to gobble down that rearing cock again.

Stanley was right. After feasting on the lawyer's gooey dark hole, he was somehow stimulated enough to open up his throat and allow that flared knob to slither past his tonsils. As the black hands on his neck encouraged him with light pressure downward, he swallowed up the entire shaft, right down to the plump balls.

It was a first for him. He'd never been able to get dick past his throat without gagging. But this time, he was so turned-on it seemed almost easy. He reveled in the feel of the giant shank throbbing in his gullet and forgot about breathing until he realized he was getting light-headed.

He pulled up with a snort and let the big pole slide from his mouth.

"Great job, Kevin! You've made me so hot my hole's begging for more attention."

The hockey star took the hint. He looked down at the dark hole to see it gaping and dribbling spit. "Sweet!"

Clamping his mouth back on that hole, he began to suck in earnest. It pushed outward to meet his lips and then further outward when he began to drill it with his tongue. Stanley maintained a firm grip on the back of the red-head's neck as he wriggled that solid black butt against his pink face.

The lawyer's moans were even louder than the hockey star's. That only encouraged him, and he shoved his tongue as deep as he could get it.

"Oh yeah! I think it's time to feed that black hole some white cock! There's some lube in my briefcase. I am always prepared."

The hockey player reared up out of that tasty hole with a nasty slurp. Grinning, he looked his lawyer right in the eye and asked him point blank, "Did you know I'd be into this? Is that why you dismissed all the other lawyers?"

"Well, I did it for your privacy, considering the delicate nature of the charges your wife raised against you ... and for a chance at this, too!"

His charming grin and broad wink had Kevin bursting into laughter. Especially considering the big lawyer was still dressed in coat and tie, but naked from the waist down with his legs in the air, hard-on bobbing and hole drooling.

Kevin turned back to the table and opened up the briefcase there, for the first time noticing how he'd scattered his own divorce papers when he'd leapt up on the table top to make his move on Stanley. He hardly cared, as his divorce was the last thing on his mind now.

He found a small bottle of Butt Oil, smirking as he thought about one of the other classy lawyers in his office accidentally discovering that in his briefcase.

He turned back to see his lawyer still sprawled back in his big office chair with his legs up and that big grin on his face. Wearing his grey suit jacket, lavender dress shirt and solid red tie, the contrast against his dark complexion only made him look more gorgeous – and his bare ass more appealing. Both his hands were down on that round ass, pulling open his juicy black hole.

"Oh my fucking God," Kevin moaned.

The hockey star was dressed more casually than Stanley, in designer jeans and dress shirt, and his clothes came off in a shot as he hopped around in front of the spread-eagled lawyer with bottle of lube in hand. Stanley laughed and wriggled his sexy black butt while stroking his own dark asshole.

Kevin's cock was so hard it felt as if it would explode. He squirted lube all over it and lunged forward. The pink head, tapered like a bullet, slid between the purple-black ass lips awaiting it and drove deep.

"Hell yeah," he cried out.

"Nice! Give it to me, buddy!"

Kevin stared down at that beautiful dark hole as he shoved his pink cock in and out of it. He was entranced by the way it sucked him in effortlessly then puckered around his withdrawing shaft with slippery ease. He pulled all the way out and stared, loving the sight of that lube-dripping pit, gaping open and hungry. He rammed in again and pumped furiously as both men grunted out encouragement to each other.

All the while, Stanley's huge dick reared up between his splayed thighs, hard and twitching. It drooled precum continuously, a glistening sheen over the flared knob. Kevin didn't know where to look, at that bottomless pit of a dark hole he fucked so savagely or that humongous black cock he wanted to jump up onto and ride just as savagely.

"I ... gotta ... get that big ... fat ... cock of yours up my ass!" he finally blurted out.

"Uhhhh ... yeah ... love to feel that pink hole of yours gobbling up my big black dick."

Even with that go-ahead, he just couldn't quite tear himself away from that steamy, sucking pit he was pounding. Everything he gave it, that hole took and more. He rammed so deep his pink balls slapped against the dark crack, but Stanley only reared up out of his chair and laughed, his ass wide open for it. He yanked his dick all the way out, and stared at the huge gap left behind, dripping lube and pouting, obviously ready for more of the same. He gave it some more.

The bright afternoon light illuminated every nasty inch of their bodies in crystal clarity. The oozing sheen of lube coating Kevin's lengthy pink pole, the same lube smeared over Stanley's dark ass-lips and smooth butt-crack, the droplets of sweat on Kevin's broad hairless chest, the beads of sweat dripping down Stanley's dark complexion, the continuous dribble of precum coating the lawyer's black dick-head. Their eyes, pale and dark, focused on each other and their savage game of cock in ass.

"Time ... ummmnnn ... to see if that sweet white ass of yours ... ooohhhh ... can take my cock, buddy," Stanley finally challenged between moans.

His asshole had already been twitching with greedy empathy as he drilled that gooey hole. There was no reason to deny it satisfaction. But what a monster cock! Could he actually take it? An anxious tingle in the pit of his belly told him he sure as hell wanted to find out!

With his left hand he reached down and snatched up the bottle of Butt Oil he'd discarded on top of his piled clothing beside them, managing to drive his cock into his lawyer's greedy ass maw without pausing. He squirted a stream of the slippery stuff over Stanley's cock then grabbed it with both hands and began to pump.

He fucked in rhythm to that slippery pump, in and out and up and down, lube squishing and spurting. Stanley's hands remained on his own ass where he pulled open his crack and asshole. The look on his face was amazing, full lips wet with drool, mouth open, eyes half-shut now with a kind of dreamy bliss.

"Get up and ride that cock before I blow!"

Kevin understood. His own cock was on fire with pleasure. The steamy innards pulsed around his thrusting shank, massaging it with both ass-lips and inner muscles. He couldn't hold out much longer if he continued fucking like that.

And the feel of that giant cock in his hands had him dying to try it out. With a groan, he pulled out. Immediately he clambered up onto the sprawled lawyer's lap. Stanley moved his hands from his own black ass to Kevin's pale white one. A down of nearly invisible hair coated the plump hockey player globes, but the crack itself was smooth as silk. Black fingers slid up into the parted valley and found the pink hole. Slick with lube from his own butt, they easily slipped past the twitching ring of the red-head's fairly snug slot.

"Fuck! Yeah! Stretch that hole with those fingers! Get it ready for your giant cock!"

A pair of fingers rooted around inside him as he leaned over the seated lawyer with both hands on his big shoulders. Stanley's thighs were draped over the arms of the office chair and his own pale legs straddled those dark ones. His ass was poised just above that gargantuan cock.

The digging fingers did open him up, and he was feeling as if he actually could take Stanley's cock. He wriggled his butt over the rearing head, feeling it pulse against his naked flesh. The lawyer twisted his fingers around inside Kevin while he aimed the giant knob right at the same spot.

"Here it comes," the lawyer warned.

Fingers slipped out and throbbing cock-head replaced them. The flared crown pressed against his resisting sphincter as Kevin groaned and bit his lip and began to sit down on it. The pressure was intense, but so was his greed. He wriggled around the slippery head while Stanley held it in place and pushed upward to meet his downward pressure.

Gasping, he stared out the window at the scene far below. The Hudson River was alive with water traffic. New Jersey spread out into the distance beyond that. Sunlight still flooded the room. Here he was in broad daylight, about to get a big black cock up his ass! It was totally liberating, along with the fact he was just divorced ... or at least had signed the papers.

"Yeah! Fuck yeah! Gimme that big cock!"

He drove downward just as Stanley reared up out of his seat. Pink ass lips surrendered, caving inward as huge knob rammed past the quivering sphincter. The shaft beyond was coated in lube and actually a fraction slimmer than the flared crown. A couple of inches of it drove into him.

"I am so fucked," he grunted out.

The giant knob burrowed deeper, slowly but relentlessly as the red-head arched his back and wriggled downward. The ache in his gut was a mixture of pain and pleasure, but even the pain was intensely exciting. With more grunts and groans, he settled lower and lower over the fat cock.

"That is so damn tight! I love it! Go for it all, buddy. I think you can take it!"

That encouragement fed his greed, and slowly he began to rise and fall, dropping deeper into the lawyer's lap with every move. He felt as if he had an enormous hockey stick up his butt, and there seemed to be no end to it!

He reached down and felt the pulsing shank buried in his ass with his fingers. There was still half to go! He flushed all over as he imagined what all that meat was going to feel like! Then he reached lower, both hands sliding down over the smooth expanse of Stanley's firm butt. He found the gooey hole he'd just been fucking and drove into it with two fingers of each hand.

"Ugghhhhh! Nice! Finger my hole while you sit on my cock!"

The feel of that well-fucked hole opening up for his fingers was just what he needed. He dug around in there while squatting down further, grunting and wriggling. More cock slid into his straining gut. And more. And more.

"You're almost there! I can't believe it! What a champ."

Fingers buried deep in that dark hole, he settled completely down over that giant cock. He felt his lawyer's fat balls nestled against his slippery pink crack and he knew he was there. With a sigh of triumph he began to wriggle and hump Stanley's lap.

Now that he had the entire thing up his butt, he wasn't about to release it. Instead of riding up and down, he merely squirmed around from side to side, feeling the base stretch his tender ass-lips and the giant knob massage deep inside his gut. The monster shank pulsed like a living snake inside him.

Stanley's hole pulsed, too, grabbing at his probing fingers, then pushing outward to allow them far up inside. The red-head leaned backward with both hands behind him and probed that sweet wet hole while he wriggled in circles over the monster meat jammed up his ass.

It was heaven, but it couldn't last. Both men were close to their threshold. Finally, the lawyer reached his. With those fingers rooting in his hole and that tight ass wriggling around his buried cock, he was at the end of his rope.

"I'm going to blow!"

Kevin rose up, allowing that gigantic cock to slide from his ass just in time. Cum spurted in an arc from the slick knob to spray his flushed pink ass-cheeks. His fingers had slipped out of Stanley's hole as he moved upward. A pair of black ones rammed deep into his own pulsing slot.

He cried out at the thrusting probe and shot, too. Cum splattered Stanley's lavender shirt and red tie. Both cocks, black one and pink one, jerked wildly as they released jets of pale nut cream. It was uncertain who spewed the most.

Kevin leaned down and kissed his lawyer. The full lips opened to his tongue. The fingers up his ass continued to massage his throbbing prostate as his cum spewed onto Stanley's shirt. Gooey cream dribbled down his pink ass.

He'd never been fucked so good! And he'd never had such a hot, sexy dark hole to explore before. All he could think of was the fact he was free now to do as he pleased. And now he knew exactly what pleased him.

Stanley broke the kiss and smiled up at him. "We should go out for lunch to celebrate. Then maybe back to my place?"

His asshole throbbed as those fingers slid out of it and he was left empty ... and hungry for more.

"Hell yeah. Hell yeah," Kevin had to agree.

DESERT GAMES
By Jay Starre

It was a hot one. Ben stared down the highway at the distant range of hills that marked the border of the California desert. Heat shimmered up from the pavement in waves, and the approaching car at first seemed just another mirage.

He'd been thinking of jerking off. It was the time of day hardly anyone ever passed by the gas station, and if they did, they rarely bothered to stop. Good time to head into the back room and beat one off.

But the car was real. It slowed, then it pulled in. A shiny jade-green Mercedes, about a decade old but in mint condition. Pretty damn sweet, actually.

The driver spotted him standing under the shade of the single palm tree just outside the station's door. He nodded then looked away as he pulled up to the gas pumps. He didn't get out, and who could blame him? It had to be 100 degrees even in the shade.

Ben sauntered over to the car and bent down to peer into the driver's window. The dude was flashy, in slacks, dress shirt and tie. His coat was on the seat beside him. He wore expensive-looking sunglasses. He was black.

He mouthed "Fill it up."

"Abso-fucking-lutely," Ben replied under his breath. The guy couldn't hear him anyway.

As he filled the tank, he noticed the driver looking in his side view mirror. It seemed like he was checking him out! With those sun glasses on there was no way to tell exactly what he was looking at, but Ben fantasized he was looking at the muscles rippling along his bare arms, his tight torso – and the bulge in his crotch.

"After I fill up your tank, you can fill up my tank," he murmured, then just to fuck with the dude, he casually groped his crotch while he continued pumping gas with the other hand.

It was a way to pass the time anyway, and when the driver continued watching, Ben pretended to rearrange the growing swell under his khaki shorts. Might as well give him an eye full!

It looked as if the dude was smiling a little, which began to really turn him on. He squeezed his stiffening cock through his shorts and just slightly rolled his hips. He didn't want to be too obvious, although he imagined how totally nasty it would be to whip it out and start pumping it along with the gas.

He was finished filling the dude's tank all too soon and put away the hose while letting go of his boner. It wouldn't do to ask for payment with a hand on his cock.

The dude was looking the other way when he tapped on his window with a knuckle.

His window came down and his hand came out with a credit card in it. He glanced at Ben and offered just the ghost of a smile. Not really disinterested, preoccupied maybe. It didn't bother the young gas jockey. It took all kinds, and he didn't give a fuck anyway as long as the customer wasn't outright rude or a pain in the butt.

Ronald Taylor was the name on the card. Inside the station, he swiped it then, with a roll of his eyes, sauntered back out to the waiting customer. This time Ronald Taylor already had his window down when Ben arrived.

"Uh, Mr. Taylor Sir, your credit card was declined. Sorry. Got another? Or cash maybe?"

The dude was silent for a moment, and Ben wondered if he'd even heard. Then, he slowly took off his sunglasses and placed them on the seat next to him on top of his suit jacket.

He still didn't say anything as he reached down and opened the door. As Ben stepped back he got out and faced him. He was tall and really built. Not in a menacing way, especially dressed in those shiny olive-green slacks and that gold tie. Ben had noticed the fancy watch, too, bright gold on his dark wrist.

"I don't carry cash. Do you have a bank machine?"

His eyes, big and dark chocolate, glanced over at the white-washed one-room station and back at Ben. They both grinned.

"No, can't say we do."

"Why don't we go inside and talk about it? You do have air conditioning in there, don't you?"

Ben nodded and led the way. He was all alone, and the highway at this time of afternoon was all but deserted. The dude could cause some trouble, maybe, but he just didn't get that vibe.

He also didn't expect what happened next.

Once the door shut behind them, Ben turned to face his customer. "Can you write a check? That would be better than nothing."

The dude was really looking him over, which was a little weird. Those big eyes ran up and down his body, definitely checking him out now. Or sizing him up. "Nice trim body, man. You look after yourself. So, how about if I do write that check? And how about if I offer you some collateral, too?"

"Uh, that would be great, Sir." Ben's eyes dropped to that gold watch, thinking maybe that was the collateral he was talking about.

Taylor's smile grew real big. He had the whitest teeth and a wide mouth that suited those giant eyes. He was a good-looking dude, with a trimmed goatee and wavy black hair cut close around the ears but a little long on top. His nose fit perfectly between those eyes and that mouth, kind of big, too, but more long than broad.

Ben realized he'd been gawking and suddenly got a little embarrassed, especially thinking of how he'd been groping at his own cock a few minutes earlier. He shouldn't have been such an ass.

Then Taylor did the unexpected.

"Not my watch, something better. How about this?"

He turned around and placed one hand on the counter in front of him. Ben's mouth dropped open as Taylor unzipped, unhooked his belt, and let his fancy slacks fall to the floor. He bent over as he hooked a black hand in the waistband of his silk boxers and shoved them down to his knees.

"Will this do for collateral?"

A big black butt waved at him. Ben's cock surged back into action, tenting his shorts and twitching. What a butt! It was gigantic, all muscle and smooth and so damn dark. A red-head himself, his tan was really just a bunch of freckles crowding each other, so all that gleaming black flesh was a total turn-on!

But was this for real?

"If you're interested, go right ahead and make yourself at home."

He spoke so calmly it was kind of unreal. And what did he mean by that? Make himself at home?

"Fuck it. Yes, Sir. I'll take that collateral."

The young gas jockey wasn't going to pass up the opportunity to get his hands on that big gorgeous ass! He lunged forward, dropping to his knees as he reached out and grabbed two handfuls of huge melon-cheeks and spread them apart. He buried his face between those massive black mounds.

Taylor pushed back as both his hands came around and seized Ben's head. He held him tight against that crack as the red-head's tongue came out and started lapping eagerly at the steamy crack – and the hole he found right away.

Snug butt-lips convulsed then pushed outward. "Fuck yeah," he muttered incoherently as his lips caressed that pouting flesh and his tongue probed it.

His baseball cap fell off as fingers tangled in his shaggy locks and pulled harder. The big ass in his face rolled just a little as that hole pulsed open for his drilling tongue. His lips smacked, and he groaned loudly, but Taylor remained silent.

Ben squeezed those chunky cheeks as he pulled them as far apart as possible and crammed his tongue up the dark hole being served up to him. His cock in his shorts jerked and ached, and he knew he had to ram it up that hole pretty fucking quick! Eating out a pulsing butt-hole like this one only made him want to fuck.

He pulled out of that deep crack with a smack of his lips and stared at the black hole he'd just tongue-fucked. Damn! It still looked tight even though the dark lips were swollen and wet. He had to fuck it!

"I have to get some lube. Don't move, uh please Sir."

"Do what you have to do, Kid. But I don't have all afternoon."

The deep voice was calm, so there was no real bite to his words. But it was a reminder of his place. The customer always knew best, and the red-headed gas jockey was required to give good service. He leapt to his feet and turned around to run over to the nearby wall of shelves. He snatched the first thing that looked like it would work.

He turned around and headed back, moaning as he took in the steamy sight waiting for him. Taylor was leaning completely over the front counter now, arms folded under his head. He'd pulled up his dress shirt so that the tail just rested above his waist. The shirt's pale green contrasted sharply with the midnight black of his hefty butt-cheeks. He'd also kicked off one pant leg, and his polished dark brown dress shoes were spread wide apart.

His humongous ass was there for the taking!

Ben unzipped and shoved down on his khakis and skivvies in a rush, nearly tripping in his anxiety to get to that butt as quickly as possible. He glanced out the station's windows, but knew there wasn't going to be anyone out there. The nearest neighbor was about fifteen miles away, and if a customer drove in, their tires would hit the buzzer hose and he'd hear it loud and clear. Regardless, he was still in a fuck of a hurry to get back to that ass.

His cock leaped in front of him as he skipped out of his shorts and underwear. Wearing just his sneakers and white tank top, he reached that dark prize. He screwed off the top of the bottle in his hand and squirted his cock.

He was surprised to see a stream of oily stuff run down over his pink cock. He thought he'd grabbed some hand lotion – but now he realized it was suntan oil. It smelled really strong – like coconut.

"Don't get any of that on my slacks or shirt, Kid. They cost more than you make in a week."

He looked up from his shiny cock to see those big chocolate eyes staring back at him. Taylor had his head craned around and was staring right in his eyes. The voice was still calm, but the look was intense. The eyes dropped to his cock, which stuck straight up from his waist, flushed bright pink and twitching. He had a really long one, although it wasn't one of those really fat ones.

He saw that ghost of a smile again and took that as a go-ahead. He stepped up between Taylor's spread legs and aimed his cock for that black hole. Careful not to get any oil on his hands or anywhere else except that tantalizing hole itself, he used his hips to thrust forward and find the spot with the head of his cock.

The head was bullet-shaped and once it found the puckered lips, it immediately began to slither between them. The oil squished around his disappearing head and the snug sphincter.

"Fuck! Oh man! Sir, so damn good," he muttered as he watched his pink cock slowly slide into that tight black hole.

Taylor lay there unmoving at first. His huge thighs were splayed wide apart and his giant ass spread open. Even though the hole was really tight, he was relaxing it enough so that Ben's lengthy cock could slide further and further up it.

The red-head shuddered all over as he watched his pink meat disappear between those dark ass-lips. He groaned loudly once he'd buried it to the balls, holding it there and reveling in the sensation of those tight ass-lips quivering all around the base of his boner.

Then, Taylor moved. He heaved backwards and wriggled that giant ass, squeezing with his sphincter so hard Ben let out a little shriek.

"Fuck that hole like it owes you money, Kid! Yeah! Come on! Ram that big dick home!"

It was a real shock to hear him talk that way. He'd been acting so cool and a little snotty. Now, he was acting downright nasty – and Ben loved it!

He did exactly as the customer ordered. He pulled half-way out, the resisting sphincter gripping his pink shaft all the way, then he reversed direction and slammed home, his pale hips driving against those hefty black butt-cheeks with a resounding smack.

"Fuck yeah, Kid! Show me what you got!"

"Yes Sir! Fucking ... yes ... fucking ... Sir!"

He slam-fucked that big black ass with all he had. The hole was squishy with oil, and so was his cock, so the ride was hot and slippery, and soon enough that gripping black sphincter began to open up. It welcomed his pile-driving shank with oozing gulps and slurps. Eventually, it seemed as if the dark hole was swallowing him alive and he just couldn't feed it fast enough.

"Come on, Kid! That all you got? Give it to me! Harder! Faster!"

"Yes, Sir!"

Even in the air-conditioned station, the action was so hot that sweat was soon flying from his forehead and dripping down his armpits. He shoved in and out like a mad-man, which meant his cock was getting rubbed and squeezed and massaged so savagely he just couldn't keep it up.

"I have to blow, Sir!"

"Pull out, Kid and show me your load."

Ben obeyed in the nick of time. Just as the oily head popped out, a spray of nut-cream erupted.

The cum hit that big black ass in a splatter of gooey white. Even while he was shaking and moaning with the power of his orgasm, Ben was conscious of Taylor's orders not to get his fancy duds soiled. While his cock sprayed, he reached out and wiped the stuff off that dark skin with his fingers and palm.

He thought he got most of it by the time the last sputters of cream oozed out. He had a big handful of cum when Taylor turned around to face him.

"Fuck! What a cock," he blurted out when he found himself staring at Taylor's hard-on.

The thing was thick and long. Not as long as Ben's, but twice the circumference! The head was one of those mushroom caps, even bigger than the monster shank itself. It was practically purple it was so dark.

"Eat that cum while you sit on my cock, Kid. You know you want to."

The ghost of a smile was back, while the voice was calm again.

Ben shuddered and actually felt weak in the knees. Could he take all that black meat up his ass? He didn't know, but Taylor was right. He sure as hell wanted to!

To emphasize his words, Taylor stroked the fat shaft of his cock a few times, pumping out a gooey dollop of precum. He grabbed up the bottle of suntan lotion with one hand and nodded to Ben as he reached out with the other hand and seized his slim waist. He yanked on the gas jockey with that giant hand and spun him around.

All at once the red-head felt the bottle crammed up between his pale ass-cheeks and then a surge of oil pump up into his hole. He was getting his tank filled – and more was to come!

He was right. The hand on his hip pulled him back against Taylor who leaned against the counter with his big cock sticking out in front of him. Ben quickly spread his legs as wide apart as possible as that massive cock-head settled directly on his oiled butt-hole.

"Sit on that black cock, Kid."

Ben obeyed. Grunting and biting his lip, he pushed back and down.

"Fuck! That thing's goddamn gigantic! Ohhhhhh ... fuck yeah!"

He wriggled his round can over the blunt knob and pushed down as hard as he could. His well-oiled hole collapsed inward, and it popped into him. He gasped, just in time to get his own cum-filled hand pressed against his open mouth.

"Now eat your cum, Kid. You're getting another load to swallow soon enough."

The young gas jockey slurped and sucked. He'd eaten his own wad before and swallowed other dude's cum, too, and he'd liked it then. Now he loved it. With loud smacks, he licked his own fingers clean as Taylor held his hand up against his face and held his big cock in place as the red-head slowly sat down on it.

With a wriggle of his slim hips, he cork-screwed the monster head deeper into his gut. He could feel that mushroom burrowing further and further up into him as he steadily impaled himself on the enormous shank.

"Sweet ass, Kid! Very sweet. You're a champ to take all that black meat up that tight white butt of yours. Now fuck yourself good. I want to come."

The cool voice whispered in his ear as he leaned back and half-squatted on that gigantic tool up his ass. He had no idea how much he had in him, but it felt like a goddamn yard of dick in there. He licked his fingers furiously and smacked his lips as he pushed downward as hard as he could.

"Fuck," he bleated. "How much more is there?"

"Almost there. Ride it up and down and you'll get it all."

He did, rising up off the huge shaft, then driving down over it. The giant knob in his ass rubbed his innards like a giant apple or orange up there, but it felt good. His prostate was on fire, and his ass-lips were getting the stretch of their life.

"Yeah. That's it, Kid. You got it. Black balls up against lily-white ass-crack."

And he realized he did have it all in him. He felt Taylor's smooth belly against his butt and those big balls slapping his crack. Just the idea of it was so hot he went wild, humping the giant pole with savage slams and shoves.

"Yeah! So good! Fuck! I'm gonna blow! Pull off, Kid."

Ben groaned as he obeyed, stepping forward as all that black meat slid out of his hole with an oily squish. He turned around and fell to his knees in front of Taylor, just in time.

A geyser of nut-cream spewed from the black knob. He reached out and grabbed the dark pole and aimed the head at his open mouth. Cum spattered his tongue, his lips and his chin. He lapped it up eagerly.

"Sweet, Kid. Sweet."

Ben swallowed it all, on his knees with his cock hard again and his asshole throbbing open after that giant black cock had stuffed it so well. Taylor smiled and winked as he reached down and grabbed Ben by the hair again. He stuffed his big cock into his open mouth.

"Clean it off, Kid. I want to get out of here."

The kneeling gas jockey licked and slurped as he stroked his own stiff cock and reached back to finger his oil-oozing hole. He was more excited than ever!

"Great job. Thanks."

Taylor pulled out and released his head. Immediately, he bent over to pull up his underwear and slacks. He was dressed in seconds, while Ben remained on his knees still jerking off and playing with his stretched asshole.

"Nice. You can stay like that while I head out."

He winked and chuckled as he pulled out his wallet and produced two bills. "Hell, I forgot I had these. For your trouble."

He dropped two crisp one hundred dollar bills onto the floor between Ben's knees and walked away. The door chimed as it slammed shut behind him.

Ben moaned as he crammed three fingers up his ass, still barely enough to satisfy the void left behind by Taylor's massive meat. The fucker! He'd had that money all along, for sure.

He shot his second load in seconds, his nut juice just missing the bills on the floor.

STEPBROTHERS
By Milton Stern

With spring semester over, Adam headed home for the summer before his senior year at State University. His mother had remarried in the last month, and she and her new husband were still on their honeymoon, so Adam knew he was coming home to an empty house.

After a three-hour drive, he was happy to be pulling up in front of the house, and he noticed the hatchback parked in the driveway and figured it must belong to one of his new stepfather's kids, probably checking on the house.

Adam pulled his suitcases out of the trunk and walked up the walkway, let himself in, and walked right up the stairs. After a long drive, he was in no mood to talk to anyone.

He put the suitcases in his room, and the first thing he noticed was how hot it was in the house. If one of his new step siblings was there, why didn't he turn on the AC? Adam shook his head and took off his shirt.

Adam had been lifting weights since he was sixteen. His body was perfectly proportioned and nicely muscled at five-foot-eleven and 185 pounds. He inherited his mother's smooth chocolate brown skin and his father's large round ass, among other large assets.

He walked downstairs to turn on the air conditioning. While adjusting the thermostat, he heard the front door open and someone saying goodbye, followed by a car speeding away. He remembered his stepbrother from the wedding. Louis was a little taller than Adam at six-foot-one, but he was leaner. His nineteen-year-old stepbrother had thick black curly hair and very dark features much like his father's, with black eyes and thick lips that begged to be kissed.

Adam remembered talking to him at the wedding and wondering if it would be incestuous to lay his new stepbrother.

"Hey, Adam," Louis said as he extended his hand. The two of them shook hands.

"Dude, what's with not turning on the AC? It's like a fucking oven in here," Adam said.

Louis shook his head and headed upstairs. That was when Adam remembered that Louis was not much of a talker, and from what he gathered from his mother and Louis's siblings, he was not always playing with a full deck either.

Nutty or not, Adam still wondered if the boy liked to play.

He headed back to his bedroom and unpacked his bags. After putting away the last of his clothes and putting the suitcases in the closet, he headed back downstairs to the kitchen for some water. His mother always kept a large jug of water in the refrigerator, and he decided to forgo a glass and drink it straight from the jug. As he was guzzling the water, Louis walked into the kitchen.

"Adam, the man," he said.

Adam quit guzzling for a second and looked at Louis who had stripped to his boxers. The boy was long and lean, built like a swimmer with broad shoulders and a six pack. This pissed Adam off because he knew Louis never worked out, but he did hold out hope that Louis would end up fat when he hit thirty!

"So, Louis, are you living here now, or are you house sitting?" Adam asked him.

"Wouldn't you like to know, bro," Louis said, and he grabbed a soda and headed back to his room.

Adam rolled his eyes and finished the jug. He filled it with tap water, put it back in the fridge and hoped it was full of bacteria for Louis to enjoy.

Adam headed upstairs, walked into the bathroom, stripped and stepped into the shower. While he was soaping up, he thought of Louis, the weirdo, standing in the kitchen nothing but his boxers, and his dick started to grow. Adam had not come in a few days, so he took hold of his favorite toy and rubbed out a big load, barely taking a couple of minutes to do the deed, and hardly making a sound in the process as he learned to stay quiet while jerking off in the dorm.

He finished his shower and pulled the curtain back, grabbing a towel at the same time. Adam was startled to find Louis there flossing his teeth. The house had two full baths, why was he in this one?

Adam tried his best to conceal his cock, which was still half hard. It was difficult enough to hide when it was soft. However, Louis paid no attention to him, so Adam thought he would take one more stab at conversation.

"So, Louis, are you working or going to school?"

Louis stopped flossing and turned around to look at Adam, who had since wrapped the towel around his waist. Then he faced the mirror again.

"No," Louis said. He finished flossing and went into the guest room, shutting the door behind him.

"What a doofus," Adam said to himself. "I hope the little asshole isn't here all summer."

Adam brushed his teeth then crawled into bed.

At three in the morning, Adam was startled awake by some strange sounds. He thought there were cats fucking outside his window, but he soon realized the sounds were coming from the next room. He heard squeaking, then high pitched moaning, more squeaking, and then Louis's voice saying over and over again, "Good boy, good boy, good boy."

Adam never heard anyone come in. Who the hell was Louis talking to? Then he heard him yell, "AHHH AHHH AHHH," so loudly it shook the walls. Adam buried his head in his pillow to keep from laughing. Once the screaming stopped, he then heard Louis saying, "I am such a good boy, oh yeah, good boy, good boy." Then, there was silence.

Adam was still laughing as he thought about his strange stepbrother masturbating and congratulating himself. Then he got hard again, himself, but he was too tired to jerk off, so he rolled over and went back to sleep.

Adam woke up early the next morning and decided to make himself a pot of coffee and work out in the basement gym, provided it was still there. After locating his extra large mug, he filled it with the freshly brewed coffee and headed to the basement.

Since it was still pretty early, Adam decided to work out in just a black cotton jock strap, crew socks and cross trainers. The jock hugged his round butt and displayed his big basket perfectly, and he wished there were someone there to enjoy the view.

Once in the basement, he was happy to see that for the most part his equipment was still where he left it.

He loaded a couple of plates on the bar and secured them with collars. He decided to stretch a bit, and when he bent down to touch his toes he looked through his legs and saw Louis, stark naked and standing right behind him. Adam immediately stood up and turned around.

Louis was standing there with his dick hanging limp but low accompanied by two big, equally low hanging balls, and he was holding a cup of coffee.

"Adam, the man," Louis said. "I took some of your aromatic java." He then turned around and headed back upstairs.

Adam was only pissed because he would now have to brew more coffee.

He slid under the bar and pressed the weights for twelve reps, and he sat up after the set and admired himself in the mirror he had mounted across from the bench. Adam ran his hands over his chest and down his six pack abs. He then flexed both biceps, displaying the high peaks that always earned him attention in the gym at school.

He lay back down and did another twelve reps. With each set, he looked in the mirror and flexed his pecs, bouncing them before doing another double bicep pose.

Adam stood up and removed some of the plates and curled the barbell for ten reps very slowly, keeping his eyes on the vein that ran up his arm. Watching his biceps pump full of blood always turned him on, and his jock was beginning to get tighter.

He put the bar down, and flexed again, doing a crab pose, flaring out his lats and finishing off with another double bicep pose. Adam then did another set of curls.

During his third set, he heard Louis coming down the steps. Adam finished the set and put the bar back. This time Louis was sitting in front of the mirror drinking another cup of coffee, blocking Adam's view of himself. 'Fucking asshole,' he thought, 'Drinks my coffee and interrupts my workout.' However, Adam didn't confront him because Louis was still naked.

"Can I help you, Louis?" he asked.

Silence.

Louis just stared at Adam, studying every inch of him. Adam noticed how Louis was looking at him and didn't know what to make of it.

"Louis, you're sitting in front of the mirror, and I can't watch myself when I work out."

Louis turned and looked at the mirror as if he did not know it was there. He stood up and leaned on an old dresser that was placed in the basement a decade before.

"Louis, are you just going to stand there?" Adam asked him.

Again, silence.

Adam did another set of curls, watching himself in the mirror when he noticed Louis standing behind him. Louis reached around and felt Adam's biceps with each curl of the bar, running his hands over the pumped muscles. Adam continued his set, enjoying the feel of his stepbrother's hands on his muscles, and he started to get hard again.

Adam curled until he was exhausted, then he put the bar back on the rack. As he looked at himself in the mirror, Louis continued to explore his body with his hands.

Louis felt his stepbrother's lats, tracing his fingers up Adam's muscular back, then he squeezed Adam's softball sized shoulders, and as one hand made its way up Adam's neck the other reached around to feel Adam's pumped chest.

As Louis continued exploring his body, Adam's breathing became heavier. He let his stepbrother enjoy every sweaty, pumped inch of him and finally, Louis's hand was inside the black cotton jock strap and going for the prize.

As he released his stepbrother's enormous boner, Louis stepped around and brushed his lips against Adam's. Adam opened his mouth and reached around Louis's head drawing him in and kissing him deep, tasting the coffee the asshole had taken without permission. With his free hand, Adam reached down and grabbed the weirdo's hard dick and was impressed with its length and girth. Adam slid his hand up to the swollen head and slicked it with the precum Louis's big dick generously provided.

Louis had managed to get Adam's jock down around his ankles, and they continued to make out while stroking each other's dicks. Louis's free hand continued to explore Adam's pumped body and found a nipple, giving it a hard pull. Adam moaned, but he did not let go of Louis's mouth. Those full, soft lips were too good to let loose even for a second.

He let go of Louis's head and flexed his right bicep while his stepbrother felt it with his left hand, as they continued to kiss. Louis obviously liked the feel of flexed muscles because his dick would swell and pulse, emitting more precum whenever Adam flexed. This in turn made Adam's thick cock swell up, and he didn't know how much longer he could last.

Their breathing increased, and the stepbrothers were getting closer, but they never unlocked their lips.

Finally, Louis pulled away from Adam's lips and screamed, "AHHH AHHH AHHH," so loud it startled Adam. Then he shot his load covering Adam's belly and chest with pints of cum. The site of his stepbrother's load on his pumped chest made Adam shoot all over Louis, who groaned while Adam was shooting, "You are such a good boy, oh yeah, good boy, good boy." Then, there was silence.

They pulled away from each other, and Adam grabbed a towel to wipe himself off, but Louis stopped him. He bent down and licked his stepbrother's body clean. After he finished his breakfast of cum, he winked at Adam, turned and walked back upstairs without saying a word.

Adam stood there with his half-hard cock hanging out and his black cotton jock at his ankles and watched Louis's round butt bounce as he walked upstairs.

"What a fucking nut job," Adam thought. Then he smiled and hoped all his workouts would end like this one.

LASSO AND TLEM
By Milton Stern

The day was getting late, but according to the old man at the ranch, the next real town in the Arizona Territory was only a dozen or so miles away. He hoped to find a blacksmith when he arrived as Montgomery, his horse, needed new shoes.

The sun was blazing, more than Lasso ever experienced being raised in Virginia. Sure, the summers were hot, but nothing like this. Lasso didn't know much about temperatures, but he guessed this to be hot enough to cook beans without a fire. He stopped at a pond, one of just a few he had encountered over the last few days, and he hopped off Montgomery, so the poor horse could get a drink and some rest.

Lasso stretched and decided he better fill his canteen and get a drink himself. He leaned over to the pond and filled his canteen then scooped a few swallows of water into his palm to quench his parched throat. He checked out his reflection in the water.

Saying that Lasso was narcissistic would be an understatement. He was damn good-looking, and he knew it, and if you didn't think he was good-looking, just ask him. He was six-foot-six and weighed in at over 240 pounds. His black, wavy hair was shaggy but fell perfectly over his square face with his dark eye brows, deep black eyes, strong jaw and rare for anyone at that time, perfectly straight teeth framed by full lips.

Lasso reached up and patted Montgomery, the only thing he loved more than himself, and his horse neighed appreciatively.

"I'll walk you the rest of the way, old girl."

Lasso stood up, placed his canteen back in the bag hanging behind his saddle, and grabbed Montgomery's reins.

He walked a few miles before stopping to strip off his shirt, revealing his hairy muscular physique, built from years of ranch work and roping cattle.

After about an hour, Lasso spotted what looked to be the beginnings of a town, if one could call it that – just a strip of buildings on a dirt road, maybe ten if that many. He stopped and put his shirt back on before going any further as he didn't want to draw too much attention to himself being so good-looking and all.

As he approached the outskirts of this town, he saw a sign that said, "Welcome to Nemtoh, Arizona, Population 69."

"I guess this is it, Montgomery. Now let's see about getting you some new shoes."

Montgomery answered with an affirmative neigh.

As he walked down the main street – the only street – in Nemtoh, Lasso noticed only a few people, all men actually, walking around. And, all of them, though handsome, every one of them, looked at him with suspicion. He spotted a young blond guy, tall, strapping and looking especially clean for someone in a town like this.

"Excuse me, mister," Lasso called out.

"Yes," the blond answered as he pushed up his hat.

"Is there a blacksmith in this town?"

"What's your name?" the blond asked.

"Name's Lasso, is there a blacksmith?"

"What brings you to Nemtoh?" the blond asked without answering the initial question, and this was beginning to piss Lasso off.

"Look, I'm not here to start trouble. I'm on my way to work at a ranch fifty miles west of here, and my horse needs new shoes."

"What ranch?" the blond asked insistently.

"Jeez, man, what's your problem? Is this some kind of private community? Fuck it! I'll just let my horse suffer until I find the next town." And, Lasso turned his horse around and started to walk back to the main trail.

"Wait a minute, Lasso," the blond called out. "It's just that we're a quiet town, and we like to know who's coming through."

Lasso stopped and turned around. He hesitated before speaking, "So, what are you? The goddamn marshal or something?"

"Actually, I'm the mayor, Mayor Bottumzup."

Lasso smiled and stifled a giggle, "Did you say bottom's up?"

"Bottumzup, and I've heard them all. I don't want to see your horse suffer … the blacksmith is over there," Bottumzup said, pointing to a building across the street. "His name is Tlem."

"Tlem? Thanks," Lasso said as he walked Montgomery over to where the mayor pointed.

"If you need to stay the night, we have a hotel over there," the mayor said pointing to another building with a sign out front that read, "Hothole Hotel – No Women Allowed."

"Thanks," Lasso answered as he continued toward the blacksmith's building then stopped to read the hotel sign again to be sure he saw what he thought he saw. He did. He pushed his cowboy hat up and shook his head, wondering what kind of town he had stumbled upon.

Lasso entered the blacksmith's building slowly and looked around before spotting a very tall, muscular black man, wearing no shirt, a leather apron and those new-fangled dungarees or blue jeans as they called them in California.

"Are you Tlem?" Lasso called out.

The man turned around, and Lasso got a good look at his face, which was very handsome, with a strong jaw and equally full lips like Lasso's, but the blacksmith's muscular torso was devoid of hair, although glistening with sweat, and Lasso felt a stream of precum drip out of his cock and down his left leg.

"Name's Lasso," he said as he reached out to shake the man's hand, "Montgomery here needs a new set of shoes. How long will that take?"

The blacksmith shook Lasso's hand and spoke for the first time, "Kinda backed up, I can have her ready by tomorrow morning."

Lasso pulled out his watch. It was getting pretty late, and he wasn't about to make it to his new job before tomorrow anyway. "Sounds good. I guess I'll stay at that hotel tonight. Should I pay you now or tomorrow?"

"I like to be paid when I'm done," Tlem said then he took Montgomery's reigns and led her to a stall where he had water and hay ready for her to enjoy. "See you in the morning, Lasso."

Lasso took one more long look at the blacksmith before heading over to the Hothole Hotel to make sure the sight was etched into his memory.

For a very small town, the Hothole was quite a fancy hotel. But, Lasso figured that they were the only place to stay in these parts as the railroad hadn't even made it this far. The manager was another handsome Nemtoh citizen, albeit a bit older than the others he saw outside. There were a few patrons at the bar, all looking a little too clean for life in the Arizona Territory, but Lasso didn't mind as he had seen enough filthy men since heading west a few months ago.

"How many nights will you be staying, Mr. Lasso?"

"Just the one. Gotta head out to a job on a ranch tomorrow," Lasso answered.

"Very good, sir. That will be three dollars."

Lasso handed three silver dollars to the manager thinking the price a bit steep, but didn't complain.

"Would you be needing a bath? We can launder your clothes also."

Lasso was puzzled, bath, laundry, who heard of such a thing out here? He pretty much gave up on bathtubs since leaving Virginia using ponds and streams to wash up and launder his clothes. "Yeah, that would be good. Pretty clean town you have here."

"Well, Mr. Lasso, just because this is a small town in the Arizona Territory doesn't mean we have to live like Barbarians," the manager said with a wink.

The manager handed Lasso his room key and told him someone would be up to take him to the washroom within the hour.

Lasso didn't realize how tired he was. No sooner had he entered the room, stripped off all his clothes and climbed onto the bed that he closed his eyes and fell asleep.

He was awakened by the sound of someone in his room. As he opened his eyes, he saw what looked to be a young man, who seemed to be a hotel employee.

"I didn't mean to wake you, sir. I was just returning your laundry."

"How long was I asleep?"

"About three hours, sir. You may take your bath now. The washroom is down the hall on the right, and I have filled your tub with hot water. Here is a towel for you," and the young man handed him the softest towel he ever felt.

Lasso climbed out of the bed and wrapped the towel around him, noticing the young man stealing a peek. He exited the room and walked down the hall and located a room marked 'Wash Room.' He opened the door, and there were two tubs in the room, which was decorated as nicely as the lobby, with a wood stove for heating water and nice curtains over the windows. One tub was occupied, so Lasso closed the door behind him and walked toward the empty tub. As he looked over at the other tub, he saw that Tlem was relaxing in the sudsy water.

Tlem opened his eyes and saw Lasso standing there wearing nothing but a towel.

"You finished with Montgomery already?" Lasso asked.

"Yep, that'll be three dollars."

"No pockets here, I'll pay you after my bath," Lasso told him as he looked over the blacksmith's upper torso and felt his cock start to swell.

"So why do they call you Lasso?" Tlem asked, looking at Lasso as if he were a meal for the tasting.

Lasso removed his towel revealing his slightly swelling uncut cock, whose foreskin barely concealed the large head, which was already reaching nine inches and still had at least two to go. "That's why."

Tlem licked his lips and said, "Impressive."

Lasso climbed into the tub hoping the water would calm him down. "Why do they call you Tlem?"

Tlem looked over at Lasso, then he stood up and revealed a hefty cock that matched Lasso's in length and girth, but was getting harder by the second. Lasso looked at the muscular blacksmith with his large, hard black cock pointing at him and tried to act nonchalant, although he had been hungry for a big piece of meat for days.

"Beautiful, but what does Tlem have to do with that?"

"Three-legged man was my nickname on the plantation. When they granted me my freedom, I chose the name Tlem."

The blacksmith then walked over to Lasso's tub and leaned down next to him, looking him right in the eyes. Without saying another word, he placed his calloused hand behind Lasso's head and pulled him in for a long hard kiss, and Lasso thought he would shoot his load right there as his big dick reached its full eleven inches in seconds.

With his other hand, Tlem reached into the tub and grabbed the hard member and started to stroke it without losing his mouth's grip on Lasso's. The ranch-hand reached under Tlem and grabbed his hard eleven inches and matched him stroke for stroke. They kept this up for quite a while without releasing their mouths, moaning and breathing hard, and slurping …

"I'm gonna blow, if you keep that up," Tlem said, finally releasing Lasso's mouth.

"Me, too," Lasso answered.

With that, Tlem stood up walked around, so he was behind Lasso's head and leaned down so his cock aimed at the ranch-hand's mouth and continued leaning over until Lasso's cock was aiming for his. Both men needed no instruction as they each began to feast on the other's enormous meat, and it was not long before they both fed each other huge loads of ranch-hand and blacksmith cum.

Finally, releasing Lasso's cock, Tlem said, "For that, I'll give you a discount on the shoes."

"That was all I had to do for a discount?" Lasso asked smiling and looking up at this beautiful blacksmith.

"I'll let you have them for free if you do me one other favor."

"What's that?" Lasso asked.

"My horse, York, needs some release, too, and he kinda took a liking to Montgomery. Let him have his fun ..."

"Wait, I can't have a pregnant horse while working on the ranch ..." Lasso protested.

"Let me finish," Tlem interrupted. "I own a ranch just outside of town. You come work for me, and I'll pay you whatever you were supposed to get where you're going."

"Why should I do that?" Lasso asked.

"Because nowhere else in the Arizona territory are you gonna find a town full of men who like doing what we just did, and you can live in my house and do it with me all the time," Tlem said with a wink.

Lasso didn't need any more persuasion and agreed to Tlem's terms, and both he and Montgomery ended up happy in their new home ...

... and if this were a movie, the next scene would have them riding off into the sunset – naked.

SCRUBBING UP
By Milton Stern

I had just come home from a business trip and was still wound up from days of meetings and travel. Normally, I would have had a martini then crashed for the night, but I hadn't worked out in a few days, so I decided to hit the gym. It was after 10:30, but they were open until midnight on Friday nights, so I had plenty of time.

After changing into my nondescript workout gear as I never really went for the Spandex/Lycra look, I walked upstairs to the free weight area, and to my surprise, no one else was working out. Usually this would bother me as seeing hot guys pumping up is inspirational, but I just wanted to get a good sweat going.

After an hour of working my chest until I swore my nipples would pop off from the pressure, I did some crunches and decided to call it a night and go downstairs to the locker room and shower. Interestingly, no one else came in to work out while I was there, and from what I could tell, only the night manager remained on duty.

As I undressed at my locker, the manager walked by and smiled. I am usually a talkative guy, but I noticed a while back, that although he was friendly and smiled a lot, this particular manager wasn't much of a talker, so I never initiated conversation. He was also the kind that never went for me – shaved head, tattoos from neck to ankles, earrings, and from what I could tell through his tight shirt, nipple rings. He was also the bodybuilder type with big, thick muscles that were obviously enhanced through chemistry (and I'll leave it at that). He did have those dark features I find enormously attractive, but his look told me that I was not his type.

I bent down to slip off my jock, and I stood up to find him standing in front of me and checking me out.

"Pretty slow tonight," he said.

"Yeah, made my workout that much easier." I didn't bother covering myself up with a towel, as by then he had a full view and what was the point? I am also very well built with a naturally smooth physique and slabs of lean, hard muscle from years of working out, so I like the attention. My dick hangs nicely, too, with a pair of round full balls to support it. This would have been a good time to put on the moves, but as I said, this type never goes for me. My being blond doesn't help either.

"I still have time to shower before you lock up I hope."

"You have plenty of time," he said as he walked away then shouted over his shoulder, "I'm going to lock up early, but take your time."

We have open showers, which I like because there is nothing better than having a hot view of pumped up muscleheads after a workout, and I had picked up my share of tricks after a shower in this gym as well.

I stepped up to the second shower head that I knew had the best pressure, turned it on and let the water cascade down my back as I faced the wall. I then shampooed my hair and turned around to rinse out the suds. I almost jumped when I felt a hand on my balls. I opened my eyes to see the night manager, naked and feeling me up while grinning at me.

"Mind if I soap you up?"

I just shrugged as if to say what the hell. He then squeezed some soap from the dispenser and proceeded to rub the soap on my chest, down my abs, back up my sides and indicated I should raise my arms as he scrubbed my pits. We didn't say a word as he continued to soap me up from head to toe while I drank in every tattooed inch of muscle on his beautiful body. Not only were his nipples pierced, but his belly button and big, thick cock were as well. I was intrigued by his body art, turned on by his beauty, and getting horny from his touch. My cock was standing straight up, thick and long, and the head was more swollen than usual.

He turned me around and worked my back, paying special attention to my hard, round glutes before he worked his hand between them and stuck a finger in my hole while he reached around with the other hand and stroked my now-aching cock.

Then he licked the back of my neck. That did it. About a quart of precum oozed from my cock, but the water and soap disguised it, although my moan was loud and clear.

I then felt his hard cock sliding up and down my crack and the smooth metal of the ring tracing its path. What a feeling, and I didn't want it to end.

I hardly ever bottom, but he was doing things with his hands on my body that had me almost begging out loud. I know he sensed my desire because he then let the head of his cock slide between my cheeks and without stumbling, fumbling or mumbling, he found the hole.

Yes, he was an expert top – a rare breed and a fantastic find. The few times I ever bottomed, I got annoyed when they would struggle to find the hole and get to work, always thinking, 'Find it already, fuck me and leave.'

He penetrated me ever so gently but with a steady movement, and before I knew it, that hard, thick pierced tool was all the way in, and I oozed another quart of precum. The metal ring just added to my pleasure as doing me from behind allowed it to rub my prostate just right. He continued to lick my neck and stroke my cock while he fucked me slowly never increasing nor decreasing his pace. I was in heaven. And, I was getting close.

Within a minute, I shot with a loud growl and painted the tiles with my thick load while he continued his steady fuck. Once he was sure I was drained, he withdrew his cock, and I ached for its return. It was over, and I wanted it to go on all night. I was embarrassed at my quick orgasm, but he seemed not to mind.

He turned me around and proceeded to soap me up again as he did before, but this time he leaned in and planted his full lips on mine. Not only was he a great fuck, but also the best kisser I have ever known. My cock, which I thought was through for the night, got hard again (his stroking it didn't hurt).

This time instead of turning me around, he turned around and rubbed his big hard muscular ass on my cock. I got the message. I found the hole with no problem and penetrated him with the same gentle but firm steady stroke he had shown me. I ran my tongue up his back and all over his neck, while I reached around and stroked his cock. He moaned with pleasure as I fucked him steadily, figuring he liked it as he gave it, slow, steady, firm and sensual. I have learned from years of casual encounters that if someone does something to you, they usually like it done to them.

He liked it.

Within a minute, he growled out his own thick load and painted the tile floor.

Strangely, we had only been at it for no more than ten or fifteen minutes, yet we had both come and fucked each other. I could have come again, but I withdrew. I also decided to return the favor and scrub him up.

His body felt fantastic; the more I felt of it, the more I wanted to go at it again.

"Come home with me," he said.

Those were the first words either of us had spoken since he asked if he could soap me up in the shower.

"OK."

We rinsed off, and as I walked toward his car, I wondered what a guy like him wanted with a guy like me.

That was more than twenty years ago, but I no longer wonder what he sees in me as long as he fucks me slow and steady and lets me return the favor every night.

THE CENTER OF ATTENTION
By Milton Stern

Billy played center for as long as he played football, beginning with peewee, then middle school, high school, and now college. For some reason, coaches automatically put him in that position, bent over with a quarterback's hands up his crotch. Was it his size? He was always the tallest – and widest – kid with the ability to run over anyone headed for the quarterback like a steam roller? Or, was it his round muscular butt, which was so tantalizing in that position. He never thought it was his butt. After all, he had a talent for hiking the ball and immediately knocking down at least three defensive linemen before they knew what hit them. Years of playing football in his hometown of Newport

News gave him a reputation, and many a lineman would try to challenge Billy, but by the end of the game, the quarterback on Billy's team would never have a scratch on him.

He entered college with a full scholarship. By eighteen, his frame had filled out quite nicely, and now in his senior year at age twenty-one, he was, as one of the cheerleaders called him, 'hunkalicious.' Billy was over six-foot-five, weighing more than 280 pounds, with a chest that measured at least fifty-four inches, biceps that approached twenty inches, a waist that although thirty-eight inches was tight and ripped, quads that measured over thirty-five inches and of course, that big round muscular butt. While many of his teammates were using steroids and other 'enhancements,' Billy had no desire to do anything that wasn't natural. He didn't have to as he was one of the lucky few who could get more muscular just from looking at a dumbbell. To make his teammates more jealous, Billy had inherited the best of both his Russian and Moroccan genes – smooth dark skin, strong facial features, green eyes, thick curly hair and bright white teeth. His hands and feet were huge, and he could palm a football with no problem.

Their first two seasons were highly successful with few losses, so the team was quite surprised when their coach resigned under pressure, and a new coach from a Southern university was brought in. And along with that new coach arrived a new quarterback. The new quarterback was not unexpected as Jerry Garrison had graduated the prior year and was playing pro-ball now. Billy wasn't envious, for he was not looking forward to a pro football career. He was a straight-A pre-med student, and he was actually looking forward to ending his football days. After all, he had been playing center since he was six years old, and all the practices were getting old.

The team entered the locker room silently the day after the announcement of their new coach and quarterback. As they changed into their practice uniforms, there was grumbling about the new coach's reputation, rumors and gossip that Billy didn't care to hear. The advantage to playing center was that all he had to do was remember when to hike the ball, plow forward and hope he hadn't hurt a defensive lineman – too badly.

After changing, they ran out to the field and lined up, awaiting the introductions.

Billy looked to his right and spotted a tall, black man with an almost equally tall, but younger, black man beside him. The older man looked to be in his mid-thirties, around six-foot-three and muscular. Billy guessed he played football in his youth and maintained his athletic physique. He was wearing a tight white polo shirt that accentuated his large chest and bulging biceps and blue coaching shorts that did little to hide his full basket. He was wearing a cap, but Billy could tell the man had a shaved head, and the hat did not hide the fact that he was perhaps the most handsome man he had ever seen with dark smooth skin and a bright smile surrounded by thick sexy lips. The younger of the two looked to be about Billy's age and maybe only an inch shorter if that much. He was muscular but leaner than the older man. His hair was cut short, and he had high cheek bones, a wide sexy mouth and big dark eyes. He was wearing a green practice jersey and matching sweat pants, but they weren't nearly as tight as the coach's, which is why he probably didn't look as muscular at the moment.

The two men approached.

"I'm Coach Clifford Montgomery, and this young man is your new quarterback, Karl Johnston," the older man said with a bit of a Southern twang Billy recognized, for they were from the same part of Virginia that he was. "Assistant Coach Frase will run you through your drills today. Which one of you is Greenberg?"

"I am," Billy answered.

"You come with Karl and me," Coach Montgomery said as he signaled for Billy to follow.

As Billy left his teammates, he shrugged his shoulders but did as he was told and caught up with the new coach and quarterback.

"I think it's important that a center and quarterback get to know each other intimately. You two will have to work closer than anyone else on the team, you understand, Greenberg?" the coach asked.

"Yes, sir," Billy responded.

"Good."

Karl just looked back at Billy and smiled.

They continued walking in silence until they reached the locker room, then went back to the room that was usually used for rehabilitation with its massage tables, whirlpool and other useful equipment. Billy noticed the coach had moved some things around and created a large area in the middle of the room with a section of workout mats. Needless to say, Billy was a little confused. After playing football and the same position for over fifteen years, he was used to new coaches, but never had been brought into a situation with just the coach and quarterback.

"I hear you aren't heading for the pros after college? They say you're going to medical school," Coach Montgomery said.

"Yes, sir, I've always wanted to be a doctor. Playing football was a way of getting scholarship money, and what I didn't spend on undergrad, I can use for medical school," Billy answered, expecting the coach to give him the same spiel he always got about how with his talents he should go pro and all.

"Good for you," the coach said, surprising Billy. "You'll have a longer career as a doctor and be able to walk without pain after thirty as well."

"Wow," Billy responded. "You're the first coach to give me that response."

"Johnston here is also pre-med, and the sexy fucker wants to be a surgeon, so I need for you to protect him, so he doesn't injure those hands," Coach Montgomery informed him. "I am not all that keen on playing pro unless you're too stupid to become something else. All that money and a broken body never make for a good combination or a happy long life."

Karl smiled, while Billy wondered if he actually heard the coach call him a 'sexy fucker.' This wouldn't be too shocking, for coaches and players usually referred to each other with sexual innuendoes and pet names all the time. It was a male-bonding thing, yet there was something about how he said it and the fact that Karl smiled and still had not said a word.

"Damn, a surgeon. Cool. I'm going to become an OBGYN," Billy said directly to Karl.

"All that pussy? Can you handle it?" Karl finally spoke, and what a deep, sexy voice he had, Billy thought as he smiled back at his new quarterback.

"OK, enough of this flirting, love birds, let's get to work," the coach said. He then handed Billy a football. "Greenberg, I want you to practice hiking to Johnston. I don't want any fumbles, none. You hear me?"

They both nodded as Billy bent over to hike the ball. The room was particularly hot, and Billy was dressed in all his pads. He was thankful he had not put on his helmet or he would have passed out.

"Aren't you curious what it's on?" Karl asked.

"Oh yeah," Billy said. "It's just that this is strange for me. I've played center for as long as I can remember, and I never had to practice hiking like this in a room away from everyone."

"You'll find I have new ways of doing everything," Coach Montgomery said. "Before we get started, why don't you get out of those pads; it's hot as fuck in here, and I don't want your parents crying to me when you die of heat exhaustion."

Billy turned to leave the room, when the coach stopped him. "Where the hell are you going?"

"To put on some sweats," Billy said.

"Forget the sweats," the coach said. "Just take off the pads. We're all men here. Hell, you've seen parts of your teammates they've never seen themselves every time you girls shower together."

Billy turned around and took off his practice jersey then his shoulder pads. He was wearing a white T-shirt underneath that was soaked with sweat and clinging to every muscular inch of his torso, but he decided to leave it on. He then took off his shoes and his football pants. Now he was just standing there in a jockstrap that did little to contain his huge basket. His teammates had teased him for years about his big balls and thick swinging dick, so he waited for the usual comments. None came. The coach and new quarterback sort of looked but were all business. Billy was grateful.

"On thirty-two," Karl said as Billy bent over once again. Karl placed the back of his hand against Billy's balls and formed a cup with the other facing up, waiting for the ball, and began, "Twelve, sixteen, thirty-two ..." and before he could say hike, Billy had launched the ball between his legs, into Karl's hands and was propelling forward before Karl knew what hit him, dropping the ball.

"They said he was the quickest center ever, Johnston," Coach Montgomery said with a chuckle as Karl picked up the ball. "He's already knocked down three guys, and a fourth is gonna grab that ball ... Coach Phillips already warned me about you, Greenberg."

Billy smiled, but he was not the cocky type, so he felt a little sorry for Karl. "Sorry about that. Let's try it again."

"You're gonna take a little getting used to," Karl said as he wiped some sweat off his brow. "This one on three."

He bent over again, and Karl began, "Seven, four, twenty-two, three ..." and again he dropped the ball as Billy hiked with lightning speed and lurched forward, but this time the coach was standing right in front of him, so he stopped just short of knocking him over.

"Fuck!" Karl said frustrated.

"Greenberg, bend over," the Coach said. "Watch, Johnston." And the coach took the quarterback's position behind Billy. "You gotta slam the back of your hand up there," and he firmly 'slammed' the back of his right hand against Billy's balls, then formed a cup with the other hand below it waiting for the hike. It wasn't enough to hurt, just enough to send a shiver up Billy's spine. "And hold them there. You should place them in just the right position to lift this big sexy ass off the ground." And with that, he lifted Billy off his feet, leaving the center to use the ball as a support to keep from falling flat on his face. The coach then gently put him back down. "That way, no matter when he hikes the ball, you won't drop it. Now you try."

When the coach removed his hands, Billy actually missed them then he realized his dick was starting to swell a bit, and some precum was leaking out. Now, he wished he had gone to get those sweat pants. He hoped that if he continued to sweat as much as he was now, his jock might be too wet for anyone to notice.

"On twenty-three." Karl resumed his position, this time slamming the back of his hand up Billy's crotch, then forming a cup with the other hand. He then attempted to lift Billy up, but he couldn't, so he just began, "Twelve, twenty, sixteen, twenty-three …" and this time he held onto the ball, but not before almost dropping it again.

"You're getting it … again," the Coach said.

Billy quickly assumed the position before they could notice the precum or the fact that his dick was starting to grow.

He really wished he could get his sweats.

"On seventeen this time," Karl said. "Wait a minute; it's too fucking hot in here." Then Karl kicked off his shoes, pulled off his sweat pants and removed his shirt, wearing nothing but a jockstrap himself. Billy could see all this when he looked through his legs. Now he knew he was in trouble, for Karl was a brown-skinned god. He then slammed his hand against Billy's balls, but this time he slid them up and down just a tiny bit. "Damn, your butt is all sweaty," Karl complained.

"Just get to it," Coach Montgomery said.

"Thirteen, four, fifty-six, forty-two, forty-three, sixteen, seventeen …"

Billy hiked and lurched forward, and when he turned around, Karl had the ball firmly in his hand and a big smile on his face. He looked over at the coach who had taken off his shirt, and he really worried about that wet spot on his jock.

"Again," the coach said.

Billy assumed the position for three more hikes. By now, both Billy and Karl were covered in sweat, and he had finally removed his own wet T-shirt. On the fourth try, Billy waited for the familiar 'slam' of Karl's hand, but it didn't come.

Instead, he felt something soft and realized it was Karl's tongue on his ass!

"Oh man, I just couldn't help myself," Karl said between licks. "I couldn't stare at this beautiful butt a minute longer."

Billy looked up and saw the coach's bare feet in front of him. With his hands still on the ball, he looked up, and Coach Montgomery was standing there wearing nothing, not even a jock, and his long thick, dark brown cock was pointing straight out above Billy's head. The coach then squatted down, looked the surprised center in the eyes, and said, "You are one beautiful man." Then, he planted his thick full lips on Billy's, and they made out, swapping spit and encircling each other's tongues. He never took his hands off the ball, and he no longer worried about the wet spot as his jock was one sticky mess with the coach's tongue in his mouth and Karl's all over his ass.

Karl reached up and grabbed the waistband of Billy's jock to pull it off, or at least he tried for the center's dick was so big and hard, it was making it difficult. Karl reached between Billy's thighs and freed the obstruction, giving the sweat and precum coated dick a nice stroking while he removed the jock with the other hand and never letting his tongue leave the hot ass in front of him.

The coach continued to make out with him, and Billy didn't want him to stop, but the coach left the center's mouth for just a second, and replaced his tongue with his long, thick cock. Billy finally let go of the ball and grabbed the backs of Coach Montgomery's thighs.

No one said a word. There were slurps and moans of satisfaction, but nothing needed to be said.

Billy's ass suddenly felt cool as Karl stopped licking it, slid between the center's thighs and flipped over on his back. He then grabbed Billy's butt and pulled him toward him until the center's enormous cock was aiming at his mouth, and Billy did as directed until he felt the warmth of the quarterback's mouth on his dick. But this position didn't quite work, so Karl slid from between his legs, stood and guided Billy over to one of the massage tables. He made Billy lie down on his back. The quarterback then bent over and with easy access gave Billy the wettest, most sensual blowjob of his young life, and it was a good thing he had a wide mouth to accommodate Billy's legendary cock. The coach stood near Billy's head and stuck his cock back into the center's mouth.

Karl was stroking his dick and about to blow, when he announced, "Who wants it?"

"I do," the coach said, and with that he bent over just in time for the quarterback to stroke his cock one more time, aiming it at the coach's mouth. Coach Montgomery then took Karl's dick gladly and swallowed every bit of the young quarterback's tasty load.

"My turn. Take it Greenberg," and the coach blew his huge load into Billy's mouth, which brought him closer to the edge. Billy made sure to get every drop, and the coach did not deny him any.

"Who gets mine?" Billy panted as he let the coach's cock slip from his mouth. Neither the coach nor the quarterback said a word; they just both went down on his throbbing cock, swapping spit between them, and when he shot, one mouth was on it, then the other, and back and forth until he was spent.

The coach looked down at Billy and said, "This is how I like for my center and quarterback to know each other intimately."

CLOTHING OPTIONAL
By Milton Stern

After a seven-hour drive through rural southwestern Virginia, a few miles across the Tennessee line, and down a very dusty country road, I arrived at the TimberBear Campground. I had read about it online and decided to try a different kind of vacation, but after being buzzed through the gate, if you want to call it a gate, and driving up to the main cabin, if you want to call it a cabin, I was beginning to rethink my idea of an alternative getaway.

Between the geezer who checked me in and the one who pointed out my cabin, there were a total of seven teeth. I drove down the hill to the far side of the grounds past what I assumed was the pool and bath house, a couple of campers and trailers, and spotted little duplex-like cabins lined up in a row. Mine was number 6 – 6B to be exact since it was a duplex of sorts.

It may have been late September, but the weather begged to differ, with temperatures in the nineties and not a cloud in sight. I heard they were suffering through a drought, and by the looks of the layer of dust on my 1975 AMC Matador Coupe, they weren't kidding.

What I didn't see were very many people. I guessed it was late in the season, which was fine, since I am not fond of crowds. I parked around back and unpacked my car. Being this was a clothing optional campground, I didn't have to pack a hundred outfits for a change the way I did for that miserable cruise my best friend talked me into taking.

"Nice ride," came a voice from behind me.

"Thanks."

"1974?"

I turned to face what appeared to be a post-op FTM transsexual wearing only cut-off shorts. "1975 AMC Matador Coupe Barcelona Edition … it was my grandmother's."

He walked over to my car, and I hastily walked around front to 6B, opened the door and took in the décor. 'Early trailer park' would best describe the room, for the cabin was just that, a room. There was a bathroom with a shower stall, and that was about it.

I unpacked what few things I had with me then changed into my swim trunks to take in what little daylight was left in the afternoon. I don't know why I put on my swim trunks since they would be coming off as soon as I arrived at the pool.

I am a former powerlifter and have continued to work out hard since ending my competition days in the late 80s, which enables me to maintain my thickly muscled physique. I am not what you would call bodybuilder cut, but at five-eleven and over 270 pounds, I am a lot of man, and I have a pretty thick cock and big balls that swing nicely if I do say so myself. I am not self-conscious about my body, but I am aware that there are those with a lot more 'definition' and much prettier faces. The best way to describe my face is that it is that of a bouncer, which is what I do for a living, and my nose has taken its share of punishment as well as my jaw. I get my share of ass when I want it, but I have found that as I grow older and especially after 'a certain age,' I don't crave it as much as I used to. I figure I have done all I care to do in bed, so if I find myself rolling around naked with someone, it better be special.

I chose an empty chaise at the pool, which wasn't difficult since there were about four people there, and took off my trunks, lay down and took in what sun was left for the day.

I was bored already.

After what seemed hours, but was only about thirty minutes, I gathered my things and made my way back to my cabin.

I was kind of tired from the drive and having put in a long shift the night before, so I took a shower in the tiny stall and decided to take a nap.

I never realize how tired I was. When I opened my eyes, it was pitch black in the cabin, and the clock next to the bed indicated it was 2:11 – AM! I hadn't slept like that in years. I was sprawled out naked on top of the bed and sporting an erection that could hammer nails.

I got out of bed and looked out the window. There was no one around or lights on, so I opened the door and stepped outside, stark naked and still pretty hard. I stretched my arms and let out a big yawn, when I heard, "Hello." I just about jumped out of my skin.

I had a neighbor in my duplex. Standing at just over six feet, he wasn't a bad looking one either. He was around my age, bald and very dark, with a mustache, a nice muscular chest – and everything else – and wearing boxer briefs. I immediately hid my cock with my hands.

"Hey, sorry about that ... I didn't think anyone would be out here."

"No problem," he replied then he turned his attention back to his cell phone. "I can't get any bars."

"Isn't it late to be making calls?" I asked while still standing there willing my dick to go down, which it eventually did.

"I've been trying to get a hold of our office overseas all day. Ahh fuck it," he said, then flipped his phone shut. "I guess I should just go to sleep."

"I just woke up from a nine-hour nap," I said with a laugh. "I think I'll see if the pool is open all night."

"The pool is closed, but the steam room and sauna are open all night. They're in the bath house right next to it," he said, obviously having visited here before.

"Thanks, either one sounds good right now."

He went back into his cabin, and I into mine. I brushed my teeth to get rid of the dead rat taste and hoped my breath didn't offend my neighbor. I grabbed two towels – one to sit on in the sauna or steam room and one to dry off with. I didn't bother putting on a pair of shorts and just wrapped a towel around my waist, and slipped on my flip-flops, grabbed a jug of water, then stepped out.

The steam room looked as if a sloppy orgy was played out just hours before, so I chose the sauna. After figuring out how to switch it on, filling the bucket with water to pour over the coals, I hung one towel on a hook outside the door, and slipped off the towel around my waist and laid it on the bench, sat down, leaned back, closed my eyes and relaxed.

I started to sweat almost immediately and took a healthy swig from the jug of water. I then wiped the sweat from my chest down my stomach and along my cock, which started getting hard again. I didn't care, figuring no one was going to come in at this hour, and if they did, whatever.

Wiping sweat across my cock turned into gentle stroking until it was standing right up again ready to do some carpentry work. I closed my eyes and continued gently stroking my dick.

I was starting to feel pretty relaxed and a bit horny when the door to the sauna opened. I opened my eyes and saw that my cabin mate had entered, and this time he wasn't wearing the boxer briefs.

He walked right over to me without saying a word, leaned down and planted his mouth on mine. We proceeded to make out and wrestle our tongues, while he reached down and grabbed my dick, and I switched my hand from my dick to his, which was also ready to hammer a few nails and had the heft to do so.

The guy was a great kisser, and he apparently thought I was to, which I am of course, but his moans didn't hurt my ego.

When his mouth left mine, I missed it immediately, until he hopped up on the bench with his feet on either side of me, his hands on the wall behind me, and his huge cock pointed at my face.

I opened my mouth, let him shove it in, and grabbed his balls. He fucked my throat like a champ, and I didn't gag at all. When I could feel he was getting close, he increased his rhythm, then pulled out and shot a big load all over my face while I held onto his balls.

When he was drained, he hopped down from the bench, got down on his knees and swallowed my cock. It only took a few seconds for him to empty my balls into his hungry mouth. He then stood up, leaned in and licked my face clean before planting his mouth on mine again as we tasted our comingled loads in his mouth.

He then winked, turned around and left.

I never saw him again.

THE AUTHORS

DERRICK DELLA GIORGIA was born in Italy and currently lives between Manhattan and Rome. His work has been published in several anthologies and literary magazines. Visit him at www.derrickdellagiorgia.com.

EVAN GILBERT lives and works in Memphis, Tennessee.

FRANCIS A. LEWIS lives in Brooklyn, NY. By day, he is a marketing, public relations, sales professional for fashion, entertainment, nonprofit industries. By night, he is whatever his heart desires. LewisFrank78@aol.com.

Residing on English Bay in Vancouver, Canada, JAY STARRE has pumped out steamy gay fiction for dozens of anthologies and has written two gay erotic novels. Contact: Jay Starre on Facebook.

LANDON DIXON's writing credits include several gay magazines and dozens of anthologies for STARbooks Press.

LOGAN ZACHARY (loganzachary2002@yahoo.com) is an author of mysteries, short stories, and over forty erotica stories, living in Minneapolis with his partner, Paul, and his dog, Ripley, who runs the house. www.loganzacharydicklit.com.

MILTON STERN is an author living in a Mobile Home Community in Maryland with Esmeralda, his rescue beagle. Check out his blog: http://gayjewmobilehome.blogspot.com/ and his website: www.miltonstern.com.

R. TALENT is a freelance writer that is still driving his big-rig, still playing poker, still living, loving and freaking it up, and is still working on his novel.

R. W. CLINGER has numerous books and stories through STARBooks Press. He can be reached at kenitorico@verizon.net

THE EDITOR

MARCUS ANTHONY is a writer and editor, residing in Newport News, Virginia. He is the epitome of all things spicy and everything naughty.

earing any underwear. "Excuse me," I said, having a hard time loo

linded by that bulge in his crotch, "but don't I know you?" "Maybe

ind of t   bout

vith Ray   God,

loser?   in?"

id. "Lik   stror

ce body   e on G

lly, he   I eve

up to t   any id

staking   e san

, I coul   ery lo

ood rac   e sw

ng with   e in s

we go   behir

ill see   in pu

ed?" he   vent t

rivacy.   grabb

hard. I

k, traci   , so

ed it, ha

with m   bing

obing, I   n cock

e sound of unzipping filled the small space. I don't know who's h

, but before I knew it, I had his rod in my hand, and mine was in hi

t to do?" he asked, his tone challenging. I knew exactly, and sank

www.ingramcontent.com/pod-product-compliance
Lightning Source LLC
Chambersburg PA
CBHW020833260626
47169CB00003B/966